A GANGSTA'S QU'RAN 4

Romell Tukes

Lock Down Publications and
Ca$h
Presents
A GANGSTA'S QUR'AN 4
A Novel by *Romell Tukes*

Lock Down Publications

P.O. Box 944
Stockbridge, Ga 30281
www.lockdownpublications.com

Lock Down Publications
Like our page on Facebook: Lock Down Publications @
www.facebook.com/lockdownpublications.ldp

Book interior design by: **Shawn Walker**
Edited by: **Nuel Uyi**

Stay Connected with Us!

Text **LOCKDOWN** to 22828 to stay up-to-date with new releases,
sneak peaks, contests and more…
Thank you!

Submission Guideline.

Submit the first three chapters of your completed manuscript to ldpsubmissions@gmail.com, subject line: Your book's title. The manuscript must be in a .doc file and sent as an attachment. Document should be in Times New Roman, double spaced and in size 12 font. Also, provide your synopsis and full contact information. If sending multiple submissions, they must each be in a separate email.

Have a story but no way to send it electronically? You can still submit to LDP/Ca$h Presents. Send in the first three chapters, written or typed, of your completed manuscript to:

LDP: Submissions Dept
P.O. Box 944
Stockbridge, Ga 30281

DO NOT send original manuscript. Must be a duplicate.

Provide your synopsis and a cover letter containing your full contact information.

Thanks for considering LDP and Ca$h Presents.

Acknowledgements

First and foremost, I want to say all praises to Allah the most high. Thanks to all my loyal readers for rocking with me. I'ma always give you my all in every book. I am doing in Yankers, NY my bro Moreno, CB, Frazier, Bongat. Chino, Baby, James, Lingo, Spayhoer, Kip and shout out to OG Chuck, Tails, Gunny, Lil YB from DOD, and Tim Dog. My BX team Juice Da Ape, Dru from Burnside, and tho Blue from H-Block. Shout Dex from Staten Island. My N.C. guys from Raleigh-Tay, Lil B, and Fiver, SL. My ATL and Miami niggas, much love to Texas and Arizona coast to coast, much love, continue to read and support. RIP to my fallen soldiers and goons who lost their life to violence over nothing. Value your life and your loved ones. The life we hear about and see on TV isn't what it seems to be. The real niggas is dying or coming to jail while the nice ones are winning and playing the cut until it bite the cheese from the trap. Make something of yourself in life. The sky's the limit; shoot for the moon. To all the strong women out there, your strength doesn't go without notice; without y'all there can never be us. To the real man out there, stand strong as family and children needs us. Thank ya. Big love to everybody. Hit me on Facebook @ Bama Author or IG-Bamattieavttar.

Romell Tukes

Prologue

Sarasota, FL

Sofia was sitting on the beach behind her beach house. She was here alone, watching the hard waves crash into each other as nightfall came.

She recently got the news of her daughter's kidnap from Lissette's neighbor who told her she saw four Middle Eastern men invade her cousin's home.

It wasn't hard for Sofia to put the pieces together. She knew about Abu Hurayra's dealing with Ali, but she was confused as to how he connected them both.

Tears flowed down her pretty face, messing up her make-up, as she silently prayed her baby was alive.

She pulled out her phone and called Ali, to only get his voicemail. She tossed the phone in the sand after leaving a message in his voicemail. Minutes later, he called back. She rushed to answer it like a middle school girl wanting her boy crush to call.

"You got the fucking nerve to call me, bitch!" Ali shouted, pissed off.

"Sorry to bother you, Ali, but we need to talk now please—this is very important. It's not about me or you. I just need a minute of your time, Ali." She heard nothing from him but silence. After the pregnant pause, Ali finally spoke.

"Meet me on Biscayne Boulevard at the old boat warehouse at the end. Come alone at nine p.m. Try anything, you'll regret it!" Swiftly, Ali hung up.

***

Hours Later

Sofia pulled into the rocky parking lot in her yellow Lamborghini Aventador to see Ali's old school 1987 Chevy Monte Carlo.

She climbed out in an Alpha and Omega wrap white dress and heels, with her hair in a bun. She looked beautiful. At first, she placed a pistol in her Fendi bag, then she took it out and placed it under her seat.

One thing she knew was, if Ali wanted her dead she would have been gone; she somewhat trusted him.

She walked into the abandoned warehouse to see boat pieces everywhere, mostly rusted and broke boat pieces.

Ali was sitting on a chair in the middle of the floor in a navy blue Armani suit, watching her every move as she approached him.

"Hey," she said sadly, as he gave her an evil look while she sat in the other chair eight feet away from him.

"What is it, Sofia? I have no time for games."

"I killed D-Bo for you," she said.

"You want a cookie, bitch, and I'm sure it was more to do with like Alexandra!" he said rudely.

"Look, I ain't come to argue with you. I came to tell you our daughter was kidnapped by Abu Hurayra."

Ali frowned.

"Fuck! I should have known!" Ali said, banging his fist on the table on his right, causing her to flinch.

"I'ma handle it, but first we have unfinished business," Ali said. pulling out a 9mm Glock and pointing it at her, but she didn't even blink.

"Oh, it's like that? Well, I'd rather have you kill me than your funny looking bitch." Sofia laughed.

"You crossed me too many times—Karma is the sister of death," Ali said before shooting her eleven times in her head. She died with her eyes wide open as if she deserved it.

***

Santa Clara, Cuba

Ayesha rode in silence in a black Lincoln Town Car on her way to the St. John Catholic Church in the heat of Santa Clara—a small beautiful city full of tourists and art galleries.

She looked at her window through her Prada sunglasses, admiring the lovely streets, old-school classic cars, and coconut trees blocking the hot humid heat as pelicans and seagulls flew through the blue skies.

Since the birth of her son, she'd been on mother duty and getting back in shape. She didn't want to be one of those women who lose themselves after a baby.

Right now she had to step in and help Ali with shitty situations with the cartels because they wouldn't give up until he was dead.

The taxi rode up a small hill, as her body was filled with a rush of excitement, feeling the thirst for blood again. Ayesha was now on her 6th passport; traveling became a second life to her, but it was never a vacation. Today she was on an important mission, and her primary target was already located—thanks to an old friend of hers who was a third eye in the sky; he could find anybody in a matter of minutes.

***

Moreno sat in St. John Catholic Church alone in the 5th front row, looking at the Virgin Mary painting.

This was the church he grew up in since he was a kid, so he came to visit it daily just to get peace of mind, especially when he had a lot on his plate.

He had no clue Ali and his crew would be this much of a pain in the ass; he was now losing money and good soldiers.

Never had he been so hard to kill, but he did respect his gangsta so much that he was willing to call a truce. He didn't care about the casinos anymore; he was more concerned about his life.

When he heard about Sofia's body being found in a small river weeks ago, it shocked him but he knew it was only one man powerful enough to take the queen out.

To make matters worse, his wife left him and filed for divorce after she caught her daughter sucking his dick in their bed. When she walked in on them, her daughter was deep-throating him viciously as she was looking at her mother in her eyes.

The head was so good he couldn't stop until he came in her throat after seeing his wife standing there with tears.

"I hope you can say a prayer for me before I kill you," a young woman said softly, as he heard heels clicking on the marble floor coming his way.

When he looked behind him, he saw a sexy Arabian woman with a pair of Louis Vuitton jeans, blouse, and heels with a 50 caliber handgun in her hand.

"Damn!" He was so shocked by her sex appeal he got a hard-on. "Who are you and how did you find me?" he asked, unaware she was the one that shot him in his ass.

"None of your worries."

"You must have killed Sofia?" he asked, but she had a surprised look because she was unaware Sofia was dead.

"I wish it was me who killed her, but I would love to talk and build—so I have to go, playa," she said, firing five hollow tip bullets in his head.

As she was walking out, a friendly priest was walking in the church, giving her a friendly wave.

Ayesha stopped dead in her tracks as he saw her face; and within seconds, she heard the priest scream at the sight of Moreno's blood on the floor, telling her to call the police.

"Okay, I will call the police right away," Ayesha said. Instead of pulling out a phone, she pulled out a blade, and swiftly slit his throat, cutting off his air circulation as blood squirted everywhere, leaving him dead in seconds.

She walked two blocks away, passing a van full of Moreno's guards eying her ass, as she got in the back of the Lincoln Town Car going back to the airport.

***

Key West, FL

Ali was deep asleep in his king-size bed, feeling a little breeze from his open terrace.

He hated sleeping without Ayesha, but he knew she had a life too. She told him she was going to Atlanta to spend the weekend with some old friends.

Ali was a deep sleeper, so he was unaware of the shadow that just climbed in his window after killing four of his guards with a silencer on a Glock 27 outback.

"Wake your bitch ass up!" Fatal yelled, slapping Ali with the butt of his gun, busting his mouth.

Ali jumped up out of his sleep to see a gun trained on him. "How the fuck—"

"Ropes and hooks, fam, what? You thought you were safe in a new mansion? And don't try to yell for them guards downstairs or you're dead—but you're dead, anyway." Fatal smiled.

"Handle your business, nigga, you're still a fuck nigga. I treated you like a brother and now you trying to kill a nigga." Ali shook his head. Never would he have thought Fatal would've been the one to take his life.

"Cry me a river, you a Philly nigga—you know you can't trust any man especially in the same field as you."

"I'll see you in hell!"

"Maybe—" *Boom, Boom, Boom, Boom!* Ali had shut his eyes in readiness for his body to receive the gunshots like a champ. But then again, he sensed the only pain he was feeling was from his bust lip. So where did those gunshots come from just now? Ali opened his eyes to see Fatal bleeding out the mouth as he fell on the mink rug, dying.

When Ali saw who was behind him with a smoking gun, he rushed to his aid.

Lil Ali handed his father the gun he got from under the bathroom sink. When he heard the man say he was going to kill his dad, he rushed to get the gun that his dad always kept under the sink.

"You okay, daddy?" Lil Ali said, as Ali snatched the gun out of his son's hand, while guards ran in the room to see Fatal in a pool of blood.

"Get him out of here!" he yelled, pointing at Fatal, then he took Lil Ali back to his room.

Lil Ali went right back to sleep as if nothing happened; this scared Ali.

***

Hours Later

In the morning, Ayesha was back. Ali told her the whole Fatal story, and she was pissed. She even put Lil Ali on punishment for a week.

One night, after they were both worn out from hours of sex, Ayesha spoke.

"I heard someone killed Sofia," she said.

Lying naked next to her, Ali said, "I heard too."

"What about the baby?"

"I am paying your father a visit soon. I know what he's doing and I'm not going for it. I have a plan."

"My father has a death wish, and I knew after you mailed him Israel's dismantled body, he would take shit to another level until he broke you."

"I knew but some things are unbreakable, and I'm one of them."

"I know, but I'm coming with you."

"No—You've been through enough, baby, plus I have help now. Go to sleep before I give you some more of this dick."

"Well—See you tomorrow," she said, turning her sore body around and going to sleep.

***

South Philly

14

Man-Man was blasting 2 Pac's "Hail Mary" in his black Dodge SRT Challenger, as he sped down the expressway, hitting 110 mph.

Earlier today he found out his little brother was gunned down in East Oakland by police on his way to college.

When his little brother was being pulled over, the police saw him pull something out—which was a phone—and they shot him seventeen times.

His little brother was only pulling out his phone to record the police contact, due to all the police killing of innocent bystanders lately.

Man-Man was high off coke as he was on his way to South Jersey to chill with a chick he met at the mall days ago.

Officer Baker was a veteran who'd spent twenty years so far in the police force. He was fifty-six years old, a white racist man with four grown kids.

He saw a Dodge muscle car with dark illegal tints speeding down his highway. He put his sirens on, as he came out the bushes where he hid every night when he was on duty.

Man-Man saw the flashing lights in his rearview mirror, as he slid his Draco onto his lap from under his seat, speeding down the highway.

"Fuck!" he yelled, pouring some coke on the middle of his thumb and index finger. He finally pulled over, rolling down his window, seeing his eyes fire red.

"I thought you never was going to stop; let me have your particulars," Officer Baker said, as a back-up truck pulled up.

"Yes sir," Man-Man said, placing a towel over the Draco that was on his passenger seat.

The cop could tell he was fucked up off something, as he took Man-Man's license and ID, walking off to speak to Officer Morris.

Minutes later, Man-Man saw both officers coming his way, and paranoia took over him—due to all the coke he sniffed up his gorilla nostrils.

"Sir, can you please step out of the car, turn off your engine and keep your hands up!" Officer Baker said. Man-Man smiled, thinking about Eric Gray and Michael Brown.

Man-Man opened the door with one hand and used his free hand to let off rounds from his Draco, hitting Office Baker in the skull.

Officer Morris quickly reacted by firing shots into Man-Man's chest, sending his body stumbling back into his car door.

Both men died on the scene before help could arrive.

***

Yazd, Iran

It was close to midnight as the woods were pitch-black, surrounded by wildlife and forest trees.

Abu Hurayra loved peace and quiet instead of city areas where one can get no sleep. His home was well-protected. In the calm cabin house in the middle of nowhere, Abu Hurayra stood over Sofia's beautiful daughter's dead body, feeling guilty for killing her by choking her to death as she suffocated. He was always against killing children, but this was the only way he could get to Ali.

He dreamed of giving Ali and Ayesha both a slow death—both at the same time—but he knew getting his daughter was a death wish and a suicide mission because she was the most dangerous woman out there.

Abu Hurayra went downstairs to get some sleep. He had a long day ahead tomorrow; he could visit his new casinos in Israel and handle all the legal documents with his lawyers to get what he deserves.

He went to sleep, forming a plan for Hadrat after she killed Ayesha—because Hadrat was a snake also.

***

Psst, Psst, Psst, Psst, Psst, Psst, Psst

Jacob took out three guards, leaving their bodies slumped. Hearing the commotion, two guards rushed to the scene, and Jacob shot both guards in their chest with his sniper's rifle.

Jacob was dressed in army war gear with night vision goggles, as he walked stealthily towards the front of the home.

He posted himself on the side of the house to see four guards talking in Arabic about their boss, and how much of a dick he was.

The guards saw red dot lasers on each other's forehead. Before they could pull any stunt, their heads all exploded.

Jacob saw the coast was clear, as he made his way into the dark house that was unlocked.

Once inside, he walked slowly and smoothly with his gun trained on each room as if he was on a special op mission, as he went into all the rooms.

Walking on the wood floors was hard because they would crack and make a noise if you stepped too hard on them.

He made his way upstairs to see a little girl sleeping in her carriage, but when he tried to lift her, the body felt stiff. When he checked the pulse, he realized she was long gone; so he left her, and went on his next mission.

"Hey, Jacob, nice work out there—too bad I have cameras surrounding these areas I own," Abu Hurayra said, pointing a gun at his face as he flicked on the lights.

"You're lucky," was all Jacob could say.

"Have you heard the story of King Pyrrhus and how he used nineteen elephants to defeat the Romans at the Battle of Heraclea in 280 BC? The Romans were unprepared for such a formidable weapon and were promptly decimated. It was all about victory over his opponents."

"Well, that's life," Jacob replied.

Abu Hurayra pulled the trigger on his Ruger to only hear a click, realizing he was out of bullets.

"I came by yesterday when you left, and emptied the only handgun you had in here. Anyway, so long—" *Psst, Psst, Psst, Psst, Psst*—Jacob gave Abu Hurayra a series of headshots, making sure he was totally dead.

Jacob took Cristal's dead body with him as he left.

***

Miami, FL

"Daddy, how long do we have to be in Philly?" Lil Ali asked with an attitude.

"Until I say so, that's enough questions," Ali said as he, Lil Ali, Tariq, and Ayesha rode in a limo to his private jet so they could go stay with his maternal aunt.

"Okay," Lil Ali said, poking out his bottom lip.

"Make sure you take care of your brother and if anything happens, what do you do?' Ayesha asked him sharply.

"Call the number you gave me, I know—I'm not slow—and rule number two: *never call the police,*" Lil Ali stated.

"Good and why never call the police?" Ali asked.

"Because they are dirty and corrupted," Lil Ali said, as Ayesha shook her head and Ali laughed.

Ayesha agreed to let the kids stay in Philly until shit died down because it was way too risky to keep them around right now with so much going on.

Ali's maternal aunt would be the kids' caretaker while there in Philly; she would watch over them as if they were her own.

***

Key West, FL

Ali had to go to the CMA Casino while Ayesha went back home. When she pulled into the gates of her estate, she saw no guards. She found this odd, so she was on the alert.

She walked into her mansion in her Fendi sweat suit. When she made it towards the living room, she saw a trail of blood. Before she could even react, she heard the familiar voice, and she froze.

"Don't do it, baby," Hadrat said in her calm voice coming from a blind spot behind the living room wall, with a gun aimed at her face.

"Wow! Surprised to see you," Ayesha said, looking at her beautiful aunt in a Saint Laurent black suit.

"You look thicker now—As far as I recall, you never had much ass," Hadrat said, looking at Ayesha in her sweatpants.

"Thanks—hard work!"

"You have a handsome husband and beautiful children I'm proud of. I just hate that I have to kill my favorite niece."

"Let me guess—my father put you up to this shit. He's using you as a pawn until it's checkmate!"

"If that's how you would like to put it before I kill you, then yeah," Hadrat said.

"Ummm, fair. At least, let me die with honor in a sword fight. I deserve that, if you ask me."

Hadrat laughed. "You think I'm dumb? You're too crafty with a sword, little girl, but better me killing you than your little sister. You see, my brother is a pussy. He uses you, me, everyone, until he eliminates them—and I may be next, but it's life."

"Thanks for the speech," Ayesha said, as blood smeared her Louis Vuitton spike heels from the dead guards Hadrat had dispatched.

"I still love you." Hadrat was about to pull the trigger, but her head exploded off her shoulders like a balloon. She hadn't noticed Jacob's presence at her back as she was focused on Ayesha. The blast that killed her had come from the AR-15 assault rifle Jacob held in his hands.

"I had it under control," Ayesha said, giving him the evil eye as she had a blade under her sleeve.

"No, you didn't, but I came to tell Ali his daughter was killed by your father, but I killed Abu Hurayra so Cristal can rest in peace. Also tell him I'll see him on the other side and I'm sorry, and to take care of my nephew."

Jacob walked out the mansion, leaving her with a confused look as she wondered if he was high.

Ayesha thought about what Hadrat meant by her having a little sister, and the news of her father being killed was too much to bear. She called Ali. He'd just texted her earlier, saying he was near.

***

Jacob was sitting in his black Corvette C7 206 ZRI packed at the bottom area near the mansion gates.

He pulled out a loaded 9mm Beretta, thinking about his life, loved ones, and future that was lonely and cloudy.

Jacob survived bad PTSD which nobody knew about, except Amina, who used to hear him going crazy in his sleep.

He killed hundreds of innocent kids, women, and elderly people just to complete a mission.

There was a monster inside of him that he couldn't control and the only way to release it was to kill him.

Jacob put the pistol to his head in tears, as he pulled the trigger, killing himself.

Ali was outside his gates when he heard the loud gun fire, and he saw the lighting from the gun blast that went off in the Corvette.

Ali hopped out the Yukon truck with his goons to see blood all over the windows, so he was unable to see who was in the car.

When he snatched the door open, Jacob's body fell on the floor. Ali couldn't believe he just killed himself, as his 9mm was still in his hand.

He ran inside the house to see blood and bodies everywhere towards the living room, as Ayesha was sitting on the stairs, zoned out.

***

Hours later, after the house was clean of all the blood and bodies, Ayesha cooked a halal meal. She told Ali the message Jacob left for him, and he was hurt but he knew it comes with the life he lived.

The two talked all night about new plans since all of the real issues were now resolved literally.

Ayesha explained to Ali that she may have a sister that she knew nothing about, and it was driving her crazy as Hadrat's words repeated in her head.

Ali got a call from Ole Bay, and he asked him to meet him asap on his yacht so they could talk. Ali agreed, as Ayesha overheard the name *Ole Bay*; the meeting didn't sit well with her, but she kept it to herself.

***

Monterrey, Mexico

Ole Bay wore Versace slacks and shirt to match, as he was golfing on his lower deck on his 177-foot yacht worth 29.1 million dollars.

He loved golfing and spending time on his yacht in the sea.

"You like golf, kid? It's a good stress reliever," Ole Bay said to Ali, as he sat at the glass table surrounded by Ole Bay's goons watching the waves.

"I golf a couple of times but I'm more of a basketball man."

"I see, I used to be as well while growing up," Ole Bay said.

Ali had no weapons or goons with him. He had to leave his people and guns back at Ole Bay's mansion; it was Ole Bay's policy, but Ali felt naked and uncomfortable.

"I called you out here to tell you Joker is dead—he tried to cross me, so he is the least of your worries," Ole Bay said as Ali overlooked what he just said. "Anyway, I want to tell you a little story before your time," Ole Bay said, pouring himself a glass of liquor.

"Years ago I met a beautiful woman that I grew to love and care for even though she was another man's property. We became lovers and had a little boy. He was my life but I had to play the distant role to avoid trouble because she was now in love with her man. Long story short, my son is killed years later by someone close to him. My son was no angel but he was still my only blood." There was a sad look in Ole Bay's eyes.

"I'm sorry to hear that."

"I had eyes on my son's killer for years and I could never get a hold of him, and he's still out here."

"Damn, I wish I can help."

"You see, Ali, you did enough already because this is the reason why you're here. The woman I was referring to is Mona—your mother—and my son was Haqq, your brother who you killed."

Ali stood up to see twenty H&K MP5 assault rifles pointing at him.

Before Ali could reply, he was on the edge of the yacht as the guards riddled his upper body with bullets. Ali's lifeless body fell into the ocean full of sharks.

When Ole Bay saw blood stain the ocean, and Ali's dead body lying there, he smiled. His mission was now complete.

***

Key West, FL

Ayesha was home all alone sleeping in her safe room that blended in with the wall so nobody would have a clue about the room. This was her favorite room, and all the camera's monitors were in there.

She was sleeping until she heard the alarms go off which made her look at the TV to see over forty Mexicans rushing in her empty house, as well as Arabians. She looked confused.

Ayesha got dressed in her catsuit with a bullet-proof vest and two AR-15s with high coolness on the system.

"I hope they come correct," she said, punching a code into the digital box on the wall that turned off all the lights in the house, as she placed her night vision goggles on and exited the room.

She took out six gunmen outside of the room, then she made her way downstairs, killing ten of them. The killing lasted for twenty minutes until she made it out

Outside in the garage, she killed eight Arabians with ease. Afterwards, she hopped in Ali's Ferrari 488, racing off. She called Ali, and he picked up.

"Ali, where are you?" she shouted in fear for his safety.

"Sorry, Ayesha, Ali is not with us anymore but I'm impressed you made it out. It must be true what they say about you. Well, I'm Ole Bay, nice to finally meet you."

Ayesha was crying, racing down the street.

"You'll be meeting me sooner than you think," she said, hanging up, pulling over to cry and vomit, thinking about revenge.

Romell Tukes

Chapter One

Fayetteville, N.C.

The robbers paced the floor in the huge master bedroom in the three-story house, in the middle-class neighborhood, with an AK pistol clutched in their hands. The warm room had Gucci curtains and a 62-inch flat screen TV. "Where the fuck is the shit at, hoe nigga? I ain't gonna ask you again!" Bundles demanded, aiming his AK directly at Pusha's head as he was tied on the floor next to his beautiful girlfriend, Ebony, who was tied up as well.

Pusha was a kingpin in the streets of NC. Although he was originally from Atlanta, this was his second home. He formed a crew in the Holly Heights project where he controlled his drug turf, and his young savages were ready to kill at his command. He thought that buying a house minutes away from Fayetteville State University for him and Ebony would keep them outta harm's way and away from the lurkers.

Trying to get a better look at the young gunmen, Pusha had no clue who they were but he knew they came barefaced. As a result, he knew his odds of making it out alive were slim. Throughout his thirty-two years on earth he'd never been robbed. Seeing Ebony cry like a baby had him regretting bringing her into the lifestyle he lived.

"Who sent y'all, shawty? Look, I'll pay double. Y'all making a big mistake!" Pusha said with a trembling voice as his gold grill shined like diamonds. Pusha had been in the game for over ten years, and he did a successful job at keeping his circle tight, leaving no loose ends in his organization. He was even able to duck and dodge a couple of federal raids in his own backyard, while they snatched a couple of his loyal workers.

"Nigga, what—" *Whack*! Bundles rammed the butt of the AK in Pusha's face, busting his nose as Ebony screamed while Lil Ali—ready to leave—held her at gunpoint.

"Baby, please tell them where it's at so they can go," Ebony said, pleading as Pusha's blood stained his white thick Chanel carpet. She cursed herself for quitting college and her modeling career to be with him even though he took good care of her. Twenty-five years old, she pushed a Benz coupé and a white Range, two closets full of designer shit, a bankroll, and a hair store she owned. She was 5'11", petite, with light cinnamon complexion, nice perky C-cup breasts, shoulder-length hair, and lovely dimples. Most of all, she was a hottie with fire pussy.

"Bitch, shut the fuck up! I'm not giving up shit!" Pusha yelled as both men laughed while Bundles rubbed his trigger, ready to end Pusha's career, running out of patience.

"You know where it's at?" Lil Ali softly asked Ebony who backed up slowly and nodded at the handsome young men in front of her as Pusha gave her an evil look. "Tell me," Lil Ali said, but she shook her head *no*. Tears brimmed in her eyes, fearing what Pusha would do to her. *Psst! Psst! Psst! Psst!*

"What the fuck!" Pusha yelled as Ebony's head exploded off her frail shoulders. Lil Ali then turned his silencer on him as he started crying and begging for his life.

As Pusha wiped Ebony's blood off his face, he knew these little niggas—whoever they were—meant business.

"Okay, please don't kill me. I'll do anything," Pusha said, looking over to his girlfriend's lifeless body as Bundles laughed so hard his stomach started to hurt.

Ali eyed Bundles, giving him a look for him to tighting up so they could get the fuck outta there because it was late and his lil' brother was at home with the babysitter. He had to get back soon because knew his mother would check for him.

"In the bathroom there is a small closet door with a latch and the bricks in all there, and the money is under the living room couch," Pusha stated in a sad voice because that was all he had left to his name. He just lost half a million dollars in Las Vegas last week, so he was trying to get back on his feet. Anyways, thanks to his connect in Atlanta; he was about to flood the streets again.

Bundles went hunting like a bloodhound to search for clues while Lil Ali stayed in the room, admiring the large photos of famous black activists posted on Pusha's walls.

Y'all going to let me live, bro. I followed your order, young blood. I got kids, shawty. I played fair!" Pusha said with glassy eyes. Lil Ali gave him a look telling him to shut the fuck up because he hated bitch made niggas who was a killer in the streets but when someone ran down on them they started shaking like a stripper on a pole.

Bundles rushed back in the room with four Louis Vuitton bags filled with keys and money.

"This nigga was holding a fortune, fam. This is big time, cuz," Bundles said, dropping the bags on the floor as his AK dangled from his neck on his shoulder strap.

"We out then," Lil Ali said and shot Pusha seven times in his upper torso. Pusha's body shook a couple of times before choking on his blood, lying stiff dead within five seconds, next to Ebony's head dangling from her shoulders.

"Come on, and why you always have to bring them big ass guns like we going to war? You act like you want someone to hear us," Lil Ali said, grabbing two of the duffle bags as Bundles grabbed the other two, trailing behind his best friend, the same way they came in. Bundles was a pro lock-smith. He could break into anything.

"Just in case we get extra company, that extra clip on your pistol only shot thirty-one rounds, whereas my AK shot a hundred— so you do the math, folk!" Bundles said as they creeped to the Honda they'd stolen from a white neighbor. The stolen vehicle was parked across the street on the dead end block. Lil Ali looked back at the yellow brick house, making sure his tracks were covered.

***

The men drove back to Fort Bragg listening to a Meek Mill album, both in their own thoughts as always after a mission. They'd both been robbing drug dealers for two years on and off, but this was the biggest score hands down, thanks to Toasty.

Toasty was one of the biggest dope boys in the city from Southgate, and he would always have a mission for Bundles. He didn't know Lil Ali; he just knew the young man was not to be fucked with in the city because he had a couple of bodies under his belt.

They did their homework on Pusha even though it was hard to keep tabs on him because he was constantly in Atlanta, but Ebony was what always brought him back and to collect his money from his workers in Holly Heights.

"Take everything to your spot. I'ma pull up on you in the morning after I take Taqiq to school," Lil Ali said, pulling up into a CVS parking lot where both of their cars were parked awaiting them near an apartment complex behind them.

"Roger that," Bundles said, playing as he looked around the empty lot before hopping out with the four bags and his assault rifle. He threw everything in the trunk of his '96 all-black Impala sitting on 26-inch rims, with dark tints which were legal in the state, but his loud music wasn't.

Lil Ali climbed in his all-red Dodge Challenger Hellcat with the widebody, black rims, black and red interior, a Bama exhaust, and HD lights.

His mom—Ayesha—got him the muscle car last month for his graduation gift. Bundles turned down the bass booming from his four twelve-speakers, not wanting to attract any attention. The Honda was left running in the parking lot by itself as both cars exited the lot, going separate ways.

***

Living in Fort Bragg was a gift and a curse because it was surrounded by a military base inside of its own city; the only way to enter was through a variety of gates surrounded by military men with assault rifles 24/7. There were many checkpoints and you needed a military ID just to enter inside the barricades. Most of the soldiers lived in the barracks with their families, and they traveled the world fighting for America.

Fort Bragg was the biggest military base in the United States of America, and it was also known as *82 airborne*. If one lived there, the police wouldn't fuck with you but there were still a lot of murders, drug trafficking, prostitution and gang violence.

Lil Ali saw it was close to midnight as he pulled into McDonalds' drive-through behind a car full of loud bitches who were drunk and singing to a Trey Songz song. He was starving. He ain't ate since his mother made dinner earlier for them before she went to work to do a double shift. His Glock 19 sat in his lap and his draco was under his seat as always because he trusted no soul.

He called his order through the intercom as the young college girls tried to see who was behind them but the tints were too dark.

Lil Ali was now seventeen, done with high school with a couple of D-1 college scholarships. He was also the only young, black, first degree black belt in N.C. in addition to being an expert in Muay Thai and combat jiu-jitsu. His mother (as well as his teacher at the martial art studio) had been training him since he was eight years old.

While he was deep in thought thinking about his real mother, Laura, he waited in the drive-through blocked in by party goers blasting music and ready to hit up some clubs.

Ayesha wasn't his birth mother but since his birth mother was dead, he considered her his real mother. When his father died years ago, it hurt him a lot. Even though he was seven at the time, he knew what death was—especially after he killed Fatal to save his father.

Now, ten years later, he took care of Taqiq and looked after his mother who was a nurse and worked extra hard. He was handsome, 6'2, fit, brown-eyed, with a chiseled body, and big braids to his lower back. He was every woman's dream, but he was taken.

Lately, he'd been having a hunger for blood. He was tempted daily to have a taste of blood; so, by robbing and killing, it fed his appetite. He was next up in line in the drive-through. Snapping him out of his thoughts, the cashier told him the amount then handed him two bags.

When he paid her, she started to blush because she remembered him from school. Before she could say something or give him back his change, the hellcat pulled off. Lil Ali was in love with Nicole—his wifey. He didn't ever give any chick a second of his time because he was really loyal to her. She was different.

Chapter Two

Womack Hospital

Ayesha sat at her desk stacked with documents, photos of her children, and a new Dell laptop she used for work purposes. She was a RN, and she would also draw blood from patients as well as do X-rays when needed.

The ninth floor was the ICU floor. The lights were always dim with a strong sour odor as if there was a nursing home on the floor. Tonight she was working a double shift due to a shortage of staff because most of the hospital employees were on vacation or out clubbing. Most of her co-workers were young college students in the beginning of their young careers, but they still wanted to have fun and party.

After Ali's death, she spent close to two years hunting down Ole Bay and his organization but always came up short. She eventually went to Philly to get her newborn and Lil Ali to raise them as a single mother, then they moved to N.C. where she thought was the safest place.

At the young age of thirty-three she was still beautiful, with glowing bronze skin, bright gray eyes, long jet-black hair, toned perfect body, and of course her beautiful smile.

She was still heavy into her Islamic religion and she taught her children how to pray, read Arabic, and understand the deen of Islam. She spent years teaching Lil Ali his fighting techniques. Even though she retired from her previous dangerous assassination lifestyle to raise her family, she still wanted them to be safe.

When Lil Ali recently graduated from high school with six college scholarships to schools all over the east coast, she was proud of him. She couldn't afford it, but she bought him a new Dodge Hellcat she knew he liked. Since he had a job as a trainer at the martial art studio, he agreed to handle his own car notes. She hoped he would go to a good college and make a good career for himself, but she wasn't going to pressure him.

Everyday she looked into her handsome son's face, and was starting to see him grow into a man, but he had a look in his eyes just like his father. She hoped she was overlooking it—the deadly look of murder.

"Excuse me, Ayesha, I'ma need your assistance in the bathroom to take a couple of scans. It's two teenagers who were wounded an hour ago in a drive-by shooting leaving two others dead on the scene." The white doctor addressing Ayesha shook his head, looking over the clipboard in his cold wrinkled hands.

Ayesha fixed her hijab she wore daily that covered most of her face, which was an obligation for all female Muslims.

"Okay, sure." She checked her watch to see it was a couple of minutes past midnight. She was happy her kids were home asleep and not victims of violence that went on daily in Fort Bragg.

***

Southgate

Bundles made it back to his hood in one piece. He was able to take the long route leading to the dirt road that connected to Southgate.

Not only was Southgate the only hood in the city full of trailer parks, but it was also the most dangerous with one way in and one way out. The area was large, with over hundred and sixty trailer homes, regular houses, a torn-down old basketball park, a small lake that led to a trail to the 301 Highway.

Mostly this area consisted of poverty-stricken people on welfare, low-income earners, drug users, hustlers, and the hopeless. Most of the young niggas in the hood were all gangbanging—either Crips or Folks—while the rest of the city were Bloods and Latin Kings.

Bundles parked his Impala next to his mom's medium size trailer. The front of the trailer looked like a junkyard with old grills, old used car bumpers, garbage, clothes, broken dressers, bed bug-infested mattress and vial bottles used for crack. He shook his head, knowing it was his mom leaving her paraphernalia outside as she always did when she was extremely high.

He looked around the dark area. He saw trailers and street lights. This wasn't normal because the hood was always live: everybody was always out smoking, drinking, playing dice games, and partying. He grabbed his four duffle bags and rushed inside, trying to be unnoticed because black people were nosey at any time of the day.

As soon as he walked inside, he saw the dirty kitchen with plates stacked in the sink, beer bottles, old used condoms from his mother, and perceived the smell of old garbage. He made a note to get up early and clean before he took his little sister—Teyana—to school as he did every morning.

He walked in the small living room to see his mom slumped over on the old four-section couch with a burnt crack pipe clutched in her hand as if someone was going to steal it. The "Good Times" TV show was blaring on the 42-inch flat-screen TV he stole months ago since his mom sold theirs for drugs. The living room was cluttered with clothes as he stepped over the piles of dirty jeans, walking down the thin hallway, stopping at Teyana's room. She was ten but too smart for her age. She was kind-hearted and he truly loved her. Teyana was balled up under her Dora the Explorer blanket, sleeping in her small twin size bed. Her room was small but neat with a small nightstand, bookshelves, colorful pink and purple wallpaper. Dolls filled her shelves attached to her walls, as well as her bed, closet, and TV stand.

Bundles smiled and walked to his room in the back with his designer bags in hand, feeling his phone vibrate, thinking it was Lil Ali checking on him. He tossed the heavy bags on the bed. Checking his phone, he noticed he'd received five new texts—four from some of his homies and one from Lil Ali. He had no service on the backroads, so that's why he got the texts late. As he began to read them all, his face went from a smile to frown. He read about two of his folks who got shot down at a club earlier and they ain't make it, but Flip and Bags survived the drive-by shooting outside the club by their rivals.

Shaking his head, he tossed his iPhone on the waterbed, thinking about the serious beef Southgate had with every hood nearby. He looked around his room to see multiple posters of his role model and father figure—Larry Hoover. Bundles' thoughts drifted towards his biological father who was murdered when he was five over a drug debt.

He had two large fish tanks that sat on two of his dressers—one filled with thirty different types of fishes, and the other tank had three large rattlesnakes ready to eat.

So caught up in the news of his dead homies, he forgot all the money and drugs sitting next to him.

"I'ma blow a bag for you niggas," Bundles said, emptying the crystal-white bricks wrapped up in yellow plastic, then the stacks of money in rubber bands on top of it. He started counting the bricks then the cash, smiling like a kid who got away with a crime. He wanted to return Lil Ali's call but he was in his zone.

***

Bundles and Lil Ali met in elementary school in the fifth grade where they had the same homeroom class teacher—Mrs. Buckham—and ever since, the two had been tight like thieves. The two would hang out every weekend and—after school days—the two would run the streets together, playing sports, bagging girls, going to the mall, the movies, and the parks.

As they got older, Bundles dropped outta high school and turned to the streets to rob, sell drugs, and murder anything to make ends meet to feed himself and Teyana.

Two years ago, the two started robbing low-level drug dealers. Lil Ali didn't need the money because his mother took very good care of him, but he only did it to really watch Bundles' back. Since then, he linked up with Toasty and he would have a line-up on niggas who was fish meat. Pusha was the biggest lick so far.

***

After an hour of sore thumbs and paper cuts, he finally finished counting money. He sat on his wall-to-wall cheap carpet, taking deep breaths, feeling as if he was rich.

Everything came out to fourteen bricks and a hundred and forty thousand dollars in cash to split with Lil Ali. He took a stack of money and walked to his mirror on his closet door, looking at the money then himself. He smiled, thinking if he should take a flick for social media then he thought against it.

Bundles stood 6'4 in height, and weighed 195 pounds. Skinny, his body was covered in tattoos he got done in juvenile last year where he did eight months for a pistol charge. He wore long thick dreads shoulder-length and six grills in his mouth with his classy coast swag. He wasn't a sex symbol as he thought he was, but the ladies loved him because of his dick game; his third leg was really a third leg.

He knew the streets were going to be in an uproar about Pusha's death but he didn't give a damn. He was war-ready and he had Southgates to back him. Not only that, but he had Lil Ali who he saw catch his first body at fourteen in a park over a basketball game at night.

Many didn't know he was a real killer behind him and he kept it that way unless it was time to bring the beast out. Bundles went to play with his snake pets he loved, then went to sleep dreaming about his new come up.

Romell Tukes

Chapter Three

Friday Morning

"Lil Ali, Lil Ali, Lil Ali—wake up, mommy said it's time," Taqiq said as he woke his brother up while shaking his arm under his Polo covers. Lil Ali was so exhausted from the large night, he forgot to set his alarm clock which was something he did every morning.

"A'ight, stop shaking me. What time is it?" Lil Ali asked while coming from under his covers, looking around his room.

Lil Ali's room was large with his own private bathroom walk-in closet, over a hundred sneaker boxes, a stereo system near his dresser and 52-inch flat-screen TV that hung from the wall. He had a small prayer area near his window where he had stacks of Islamic books and Muslim oils. The wall-to-wall carpet made the room look and feel more comfortable as the smell of incense filled the hall-ways.

"Time for breakfast," he said in his kiddish voice, dressed in his school uniform, a white-collar shirt, black slacks and shoes plus his kufi hat. Taqiq had light-brown skin and gray eyes like his mom, long hair, and a swag he got from his brother. He was very well advanced for a kid his age but everybody loved him, including his teachers, neighbors, and school mates.

"Okay, I'm up now," Lil Ali said, getting up, sliding in his Gucci slippers, looking at his brother staring at him as if he was thinking something.

"I came in here last night but you weren't here," Taqiq said, being nosey.

"What I tell you about coming into my room when I'm not here?" Lil Ali said in a stern tone as his little brother looked sad knowing his big brother was mad.

"I—I—I'm sorry. I just wanted to check on ya. Don't tell mommy," Taqiq said, sitting on the edge of the king-size bed.

"I won't but you want to go out later to Chucky Cheese with Teyana?" Lil Ali asked while putting on his Adidas tracksuit and Nike shoes.

"Ugh—man, why Teyana? She get on my nerves, she follow me around all day in school. I don't like her," Taqiq started with a sour facial expression as Lil Ali laughed and went to brush his teeth, preparing to do *wudu* for his morning prayer.

"Stop it, Taqiq, she looks at you as her friend so you need to look after her. That's Bundles' sister. She a good girl but let me find out you like her," Lil Ali said, looking at himself in the mirror.

"Ewwwww—she is annoying," Taqiq said.

"I don't care. She coming. Now get out so I can use the bathroom and pray, and tell mommy I'll be down in a second," Lil Ali said as Taqiq left the room.

***

Lil Ali took a piss and made *wudu. He washed* his hands, rinsed his mouth out, his nose, washed his face, his arms then his head, ears, right foot, and left foot.

He walked back in his room and faced the east to begin his prayer as he did every morning. He was born and raised as a Muslim, and the *deen* was all he knew besides his new hobby—killing. He knew living a double life could have a bad effect, but he knew by repenting he was being forgiven.

After his prayer, he grabbed his cell phone off his charger behind his headboard. He had six missed calls—two from Bundles, two from his mom, and two from wifey.

"Damn! I forgot to hit Bundles," he said loudly as if he was talking to someone else as he left his room, walking downstairs into the kitchen. The two-story house was very spaced upstairs and downstairs, four rooms but one was used for prayer, reading and meditation. The furnishings consisted of rosewood furniture against cream-colored walls, and curtains with touches of dark blue and flannel gray outlines. Also, there were photos of him and Taqiq as well as their father when he was living in Miami, Vegas and there was even a large photo of their grandma—Mona—who was killed years ago.

Nobody was allowed to walk in the house with their shoes on because thick soft Italian carpet covered the whole house besides the kitchen where the marble tiles covered the area.

Once in the kitchen, he smelled the strong scent of eggs, sausages, hash browns, and pancakes, as his mom—clad in her work clothes—was cooking.

"As-salaam-alaikum," she said, not looking behind her, still alert from her old life.

"Wai alaikum-salaam. You didn't have to cook, mom," he said, sitting on a stool next to Taqiq.

"It's good I was up plus we got to train at eleven so just be back on time. I'ma take a nap, and why didn't ya call me back last night?" she said, turning off the stove as the food was done.

"I was sleep," he said as she looked at him with her deep gray eyes. Taqiq kicked his brother's foot, letting him know it's not nice to lie to mommy. Lil Ali kicked his foot back, letting him know to shut up.

"Okay, eat up, I'ma go take a nap," she said, wondering why the two of them were face fighting.

"Why you not eating?" Lil Ali asked as they began to eat, seeing she only made two plates.

"I'm good, just tired. Please make sure he get to school on time this time," she said sharply.

"I will," Lil Ali replied, enjoying his breakfast as he poured himself a glass of OJ, wondering what today's training consisted of because normally it was rough. Sometimes the two would run miles, do hours of cardio, strength, sprints, gun ranges, sword fights in the woods, alert training, balance training and even meditation. He'd never seen anybody in shape as Ayesha was; she was toned with a six-pack and very fast.

"Here is some lunch money," she said, going into her Fendi purse, pulling out ten dollars.

"I got it, mom," Lil Ali said, stopping her. She gave him a funny look, knowing most of his checks go to his car notes or phone bill.

"Okay—love y'all," she said, walking upstairs to shower and nap before her daily workout with her son.

**

Lil Ali and Taqiq walked down the two steps outside of the house to see the sun exposed through the deep clouds as the warm heat took over the morning humidity. Their small yard, which was neatly cut, matched up with the rest of the block. The neighborhood was middle-class.

His Dodge—with five percent tints—was parked next to Ayesha's new sleek all-black Audi A7.

"You shouldn't lie to mommy," Taqiq said as he tossed his Dragon Ball Z backpack in the backseat, climbing inside his brother's car which he loved.

"You should mind your business," Lil Ali said, giving him twenty dollars, pulling out of the driveway and listening to a Migos album, knowing full well the American hip hop trio were Taqiq's favorite rappers.

Minutes later they pulled up behind a few school buses at school. They saw kids running around everywhere dressed in their uniforms.

"Be good today and I'll be back to get you later," Lil Ali said, checking the time on his installed digital screen in his dashboard that was used for a GPS, rearview mirror, and his radio.

"I will and I love you," Taqiq replied in his little voice, hopping out with his backpack, closing the door behind him.

**

Lil Ali passed the Southgate sign to see over twenty teens posted up; most of them had guns and drugs on them while the rest were skipping school.

A couple of chicks and goons looked at the red Hellcat, wondering who was behind the tints. So, he rolled down his window a little just so he wouldn't get mistaken for a cop trying to slide on them.

When they saw who it was, they focused their attention somewhere else as the women stared even harder, getting wet. Lil Ali was the talk of the women and goons, but people feared Bundles right-hand man whom they knew nothing about except he was a handsome killer.

Once he saw the black Impala, he parked next to it, looking around, shaking his head at how dirty Southgate was. He climbed out and walked inside without knocking as he always did because he was like family and Bundles' mom—Macy—ain't care.

"Yo, Bundles!" Lil Ali yelled over the loud TV in the living room playing the news as nobody was there. He looked at the TV to see two murders of a drug dealer and his girlfriend but no suspects were found, no witness, or nothing. However, when he saw Pusha's mug shot and a picture of Ebony, a deep relief came over him.

Bundles walked out from the back shirtless, showing his tattoos covering his body, smoking a blunt with a snake dancing around his frail neck.

"What's up, bro? Come to the back before my thirsty ass mom comes back," Bundles said, smiling ear to ear, taking the snake into his hands.

"Put that shit up, dawg," Lil Ali said, closing Bundles' room door, smelling weed smoke in thick clouds.

"Chill, I'ma put him up, scared nigga," Bundles said, putting the snake in the tank." After a pause, rubbing his ashy hands, he said, "We hit big, man."

"How much, dawg?" Lil Ali replied, sitting in the loveseat in the far corner of the room.

"Seven keys apiece and seventy thousand apiece," Bundles said, bringing out the drugs and money from his closet.

"Damn, look, I gotta hurry. Give my bricks to Big Ray and tell him twenty apiece," Lil Ali said, grabbing Bundles' YMCA bookbag, throwing his money in the bag. He'd never seen this much money.

"Okay, I got you," Bundles said.

"After school we taking Teyana and Taqiq to Chucky Cheese.

"Alright, cool, I gotta clear this shit and take her shopping also," he said, walking his friend out so he could call over one of his hotties to celebrate. As soon as Lil Ali stepped in the living room, Macy was staring right at him with her big eyes and wild hair.

Macy was thirty-eight with dark skin, a nice slim body, dark wide eyes, long hair that was always unkempt, dirty fingernails, and thick lips. For a crack head she was still cute, but she gave up on herself. Her pussy was still good and she had the meanest head game in Southgate if your money was right.

"Let me get some money, boy," she said in her country accent, looking Lil Ali up and down, thinking what she would do to his young ass if he wasn't her son's friend because she didn't have an age limit.

"I'm broke, Macy, next time I got you."

"How you broke driving a Mustang?" she said with her hand on her slim hip, sucking her rotten teeth she couldn't afford to get taken care of.

"It's not a Mustang—it's a Hellcat," Lil Ali said, correcting her.

"Whatever, and you going to the YMCA at nine o'clock?" she said, wondering what's in the bag.

"Mom, mind your damn business," Bundles yelled while on the phone as Lil Ali slid out the front door.

"Boy, shut up before I kick your ass out. And give me some money, you broke ass nigga!" she yelled, seeing Lil Ali's car pulling off, licking her lips and wondering if he was packing.

Chapter Four

Fayetteville State University

Nicole was sitting in the back of her philosophy class listening to professor Wrath give a lecture about a famous Greek writer as he paced the lower floor among the sixty students.

Listening to lessons and texting Lil Ali under her desk was a task she learned to do since middle school but today her mind wasn't really on school. She ain't seen her boo in a week and she missed him but she was starting to get irritated.

She felt someone staring at her, so she looked behind her to see one of the school basketball stars eyeing her as always. She sucked her teeth and checked her watch.

At five foot four, a hundred and thirty pounds with vital statistics of 36-26-42, she was a sight to see. She'd won beauty competitions, and model agencies were begging for her but she refused. She was a redbone with a white mother and black father. She exercised daily, so her stomach was flat. Her daily exercise gave her a toned body and a phat ass. She had long jet-black hair with brown streaks, but her best feature was her bright green and orange eyes. Already eighteen, she was focused on a career as a writer and news reporter.

FSU was a good school but the only reason she picked it over Ohio State and Duke University was to be close to her man. She lived in the dorm with her crazy roommate—Nancy—from Texas who was a party girl majoring in Business Management.

She spent most of her time at her mom's house studying and going back and forth to work in a Nordstrom clothing store.

The professor was acting out a play in front of the class as he always did. Nicole thought back to the first time she and Lil Ali met.

They were both ten years old at the time. She was in the park down the street from her house in Tiffany Pines. Lil Ali was playing basketball with his shirt off showing his little muscles as she watched him play, wondering who he was because she had a crush on him.

The basketball rolled off the court toward her little feet while she was on the swings. Before she could even pick up the ball, he was in front of her with a smile that made her smile back. He introduced himself and asked her out. Since then the two had been a couple, and he took her virginity on prom night.

Her mom hated Lil Ali not because he was black but because she was Jewish and was heavy in her religion, and she tried to instill that into her daughter. When she found out he was a Muslim, she caused a big scene telling her to stay away because he was a terrorist.

Lil Ali taught Nicole about his religion. She even read the Qu'ran daily and she understood it, but she knew her mom was just misguided. She even fasted with him during one Ramadan period, and she liked it; not only was it a regimen of discipline but it was healthy.

This was her freshman year and she was already considered one of the smartest freshmen in the school at Ivy legend status. She wished Lil Ali would go to college because he was very smart. Each time she brought up the idea of him going to college, his response was: "When the time comes."

She knew he was in the streets. She wasn't dumb or naive. She saw him with guns daily, but she knew he had to protect himself; it was the code. One of her friends told her that her boyfriend said the streets called Lil Ali the Grim Reaper because he had a couple of bodies, but Nicole didn't believe the rumors.

The professor ended the class as students rushed out preparing for their next classes or study groups somewhere on campus. She threw all her notes in her Gucci, carrying the bag as she placed her Gucci shades over her face. Her off-white dress hugged her body tightly as her pretty toes were exposed in her six-inch heels, as she followed the crowd out the class.

Today was Friday, so she knew Lil Ali and Ayesha would be going to Muslim service at one o'clock as they always did. She liked Ayesha. She found her so pretty and nice. When she first met her, she thought she was Lil Ali's sister because she looked so young.

Nicole made it to the parking lot where her all-black Kia Stinger GT2 AWD was. She tossed her bags in the back, checking to see if Lil Ali texted but it was only her best friend. She played her Monica album and pulled out her parking space, going to wait on Lil Ali at his house.

***

Jummah

The mosque was a small temple located on the outskirts of Fort Bragg where Muslim men and women would come to pray. As soon as you walked inside, you had to take off your shoes and place them on the shoe rack. The prayer area was half the size of a football field filled with black Muslims, white, Spanish, Arabians, Africans—all dressed in Muslim attire. The men sat Indian-style in the front while the women and children sat in the back, all listening to the Imam give his Friday sermon speech then lead the community in prayer.

Ayesha had been coming here since she moved to Fayetteville. The Imam was an African brother from Cape Town. She sat in the back with Taqiq quietly with the rest of the women and kids.

Every Friday she would take him out of school for a half day so he could attend his religious service, and the school was okay with it. She was a little distracted today for many reasons, but the main one was Lil Ali. Today she went to pay rent and all the bills until she was notified that all her bills were covered for a whole period of a year. When she asked how, they said her son took care of it on her behalf which shocked and confused her.

She appreciated his help but her job paid her very well. That's how she was able to push a new Audi and take care of all of them. She hoped he wasn't selling drugs because she was totally against that, but she knew that was not the case because she raised him better than that.

Knowing what type of individual his father was, she hoped he could become a better man. She knew she'd done her best.

After Jummah, she took Taqiq to go get ice cream and some new Xbox games, wondering why her other son missed Jummah and he better have a good excuse because Jummah was mandatory.

***

Lil Ali stood at his favorite river bank, staring off into the dirty water, watching fishermen fish in the deep end of the river.

This was his quiet place. Only two people know about this spot, and that was Ayesha and Nicole. It was his getaway when he needed to think.

He thought about his dream career as he wanted to put that on the backburner for now because he had other shit on his mind.

He wanted to stock up enough money to open a new mosque, and a martial art studio bigger than the one he worked at. He needed time alone to think clearly about robbing and killing and risking going to jail. He hated gang crimes with other niggas, but he trusted Bundles.

"So this is where my boo been hiding since he hasn't been returning my calls. I should have known to come down here," Nicole said, standing behind him with her arms crossed as the wind from the river made her nipples hard. Lil Ali looked behind him to see her looking sexy in her dress showing her blue manicured toes.

"How you find me? And you look nice," he replied.

"I just saw your mom and she looked pissed you ain't go to Jummah," Nicole said in an apprehensive voice, letting him know he was in trouble. As she walked in front of him, he grabbed her waist.

"I'll talk to her but sorry for the missed calls. I was tied up," he said, looking into her colorful eyes, pushing her long hair behind her ears.

"I miss you," she said softly, kissing his soft lips then turning to look at the river and the cloudy blue sky.

"I miss you more, babe, and don't dress like this. You know I can't control myself," he said, hugging her from behind on her phat soft ass.

"That's why I wore it for you, boo, you know that. But I gotta go home, change, then go to work and come back home to study for my first exams." Nicole took a deep breath.

"I gotta go train at the studio in two hours then talk to my mom but I'm trying to get some loving soon," he said, sucking her soft neck that smelled like Gucci perfume, as she normally smelled.

"Yea, too bad I'm on my period so no sucking or fucking for you, buddy," she said in her sweet soft voice.

"Says who?" he said.

"Uck, you nasty boy!" she said, hitting him on his solid chest. His phone went off; when he saw it was Bundles, he paid it no mind. That would be his next step before work.

"I gotta go but I love you," she said, passionately kissing him before she walked off leaving him alone because she knew her limits as his wifey and friend.

Romell Tukes

Chapter Five

Bundles stood over on the edge of his bed naked as him and G-Loc ran a train on young Bonica, the neighborhood freak.

"Umm, shit! Yea, bitch, suck that dick!" Bundles moaned, looking at Bonica bop her head up and down on his dick as her thick lips sucked while deep-throating as her body rocked back and forth while G-Loc fucked her from behind.

"Ohh." Bonica moaned as G-Loc was ramming his dick into her pussy that had a loose grip.

Bundles' room was dark as the curtains were closed while a strong musk scent filled the air for the last hour as both men fucked her in every way possible. Bundles was forcing her head, feeling her thick braids as he shoved his dick deeper down her throat, making her take every inch.

"Oh-h-h fu-c-k—that dickkk feels gooddd!" she screamed as G-Loc started fucking her asshole, using his semen as lube as she threw her ass back, loving it and taking it like a champ.

"I'm cumming," Bundles said, nutting in her mouth as she swallowed every drop while G-Loc was fucking her so rough she almost fell off the bed.

"Uhmmm, shit!" G-Loc said, nutting on her wide ass while fingering her hairy, bushy pussy.

"How was I?" Bonica asked, standing up, showing her double-D breasts and wide hips with her little gut which was baby fat from her baby she had six months ago, but she was still cute, dark-skinned and thick, with a baby face.

"I had better, but you gotta go!" Bundles said, tossing her tank top and blouse at her while he got dressed.

"Damn, it's like that?" she said, smelling a scent of her pussy, knowing she had to go wash up.

"I'ma be back later, folk," G-Loc said, throwing on his white tee over his big belly. He was close to three hundred pounds and ugly with small dreads. Seventeen years of age, G-Loc was a crip and a certified shooter. He was a loyal nigga.

Once everybody left, Bundles got a call from Toasty telling him to come outside. Bundles threw on a tank top and a pair of Nike sweatpants and Air Force 1s.

***

Toasty was leaned back in the driver seat of his all-white Porsche Panamera with dark tints and custom interior. The car was fresh off the lot; it still had the new car scent and paper rugs on the floor.

Hood rich was the best way to describe Toasty. He was the connect around the city and he'd been in the game for twenty years. He was thirty-five now. Southgate was his hood where he grew up at and where his goons was at as his security, and Bundles was his main hitter.

Toasty played chess in the streets like a champ. He used niggas, set niggas up, kept his enemy close and he played for keeps. He was short, brown-skinned, with a missing front tooth and missing dreads with a receding hairline. He had three beautiful baby mothers who were all sac chasers.

Bundles climbed in the passenger seat looking around as the misty warm air hit his chest before closing the door.

"What's hoppin', youngin'?" Toasty said, giving him a dab, watching the traffic flow all through the trailer parks Lil Ray ran. He used to supply Lil Ray because that's his little cousin but he figured lately he was getting it from his pops—Big Ray.

"Ain't shit, bro, just on a paper chase, folk," Bundles said, admiring the leather dashboard, peanut butter seats, and the heated seats.

"I heard about the Pusha situation. Damn, y'all boys did that shit like pros but I know y'all come up. Look, I got a new position for you," Toasty said, looking at him seriously.

"What?" he replied, ready.

"There is a nigga name T-Money from Holly Heights projects. He been moving weight for years. He got a crew but they ain't on shit. I got his mother's info and she stay on 251 Roamey Road at the end of the block. Every Sunday he drops money and drugs off. I don't know what they got going on but I know he get to that bag."

"A'ight, I'll call you when it's all clear," Bundles said as he was leaving.

"One more thing—make sure you take that Ali kid with you. Word on the street is he's an animal with that pistol, and I like his work," Toasty stated as Bundles nodded in agreement.

Toasty pulled off thinking about the Ali kid he knew nothing about except the two bodies he caught last year in broad daylight. Nobody knew the cause of the shooting but the witness refused to say a word as Lil Ali walked off smoothly after the shooting. Toasty liked his style. He never said a word to Lil Ali but he knew he could be a strong figure in his chess game.

***

Lil Ali pushed the speed demand down the highway while he talked to his mother on his speaker phone plugged into his sound system. Once he ended the call, he got off the highway, entering Southgate to see the hood flooded with blue and black flags as if they were filming a gangland documentary.

He parked next to Bundles' Impala and hopped out in his Paris jeans, Versace top and Versace loafers to match. He bought a ton of designer clothes from the mall for him and his brother the other day.

As soon as he started walking, a gang of girls ran up to him all dressed in skirts, tight jeans, showing tits, stomach, legs, cameltoes, and ass cheeks hanging out.

"Excuse me but you got a girl? I see you all the time but you act like you're too good for a bitch," the cutest girl of the six said, standing in front of him, looking at his Hermès belt and designer gear.

"I'm good, shorty. I'm sure it's enough niggas out here for you and your friends," Lil Ali stated as she sucked her teeth.

"I don't want them. I want you," she said as she flashed her light brown eyes. Lil Ali walked off and laughed, going into Bundles' crib as the girls walked off talking shit.

"Damn, took you long enough!" Bundles said, sitting on the couch rolling up a swisher sweet cigar full of lush.

"You also smoking that damn shit, my nigga. I thought you quit?" Lil Ali asked while covering his nose, taking a seat, listening to a YouTube video of some of his ops closing Southgate from their long ongoing beef with the Villie niggas.

"Did you give them keys to Lil Ray?" Lil Ali asked.

"Yea, nigga, he said he got that money for you but listen—we got bigger fish to fry, dawg. Toasty came by a minute ago and he got a new lick for us—a nigga name T-Money," said Bundles in a choking voice.

"A'ight and what?" Lil Ali said, wondering what type of games he was playing, trying to form a clean-up crew.

"Shit, cuz, this lame nigga holding, bruh," he replied.

"You got a line on him?" Lil Ali asked.

"Of course—his mama house," Bundles said, putting out his blunt.

"I'ma go home, and tell Lil Ray to meet me at Pizza Hut in two hours. I ain't calling his phone," Lil Ali said, as he stood to leave, then he saw Bundles' AR-15 and AK behind his door.

"A'ight, nigga, I'll hit you later and be ready tomorrow. I'ma do some homework tonight," Bundles said, going back to his video of his ops.

***

The heat was starting to pick up in the city. Lil Ali parked next to Ayesha's Audi. The sun was going down as a bright orange took over the skyline like a wildfire.

As soon as he walked into his house, he smelled sandalwood incense coming from the living room. Ayesha was sitting barefoot on a prayer rug, Indian-style, reading an Islamic book. The living room had no TV, only nice expensive furniture, book shelves in all four corners filled with Islamic books, a computer and desk, with portraits of sunsets, oceans, mountains, and nature to give the room an outside feeling.

"As-salaam-alaikum," she said, looking at him.

"Walaikum Assalam," he replied, taking off his designer shoes, neatly putting them near the door next to her heels.

"Nicole came back minutes ago to say hi and told me you were at the river. There is no damn excuse why you wasn't there at Jummah," she said in a tone that he knew wasn't to be fucked with.

"Sorry, got a lot on my mind. Won't happen again," he said.

"You should repent to Allah, not me, but what's going on with you? And don't give me no bullshit. I know you're becoming a man and you will make choices right and wrong but you don't have to do wrong or be in the streets. I work hard so you can live a decent life, but the life you choose—be able to live and die for it. You know right from wrong and Allah sees all. I see so much of your father in you. That's what I'm scared of." Ayesha got up, putting her incense in place.

"I'm okay, mom, nothing to worry about. Just trying to help you raise Taqiq and think of a business I can set up because I don't want to work for a white man. I want to hire one. I'm not going to college as of yet, not ready. I want to help you and open up my own mosque and martial art studio." Lil Ali looked serious.

Ayesha listened silently. She wanted him to go to college and make something of himself, but his life was his life.

"I understand but no matter what, never abandon your *deen*, your blood and honor, as well as your oath to Allah and if you want to be your own boss then go for it. We need more strong young black men like you, son." Looking at him, Ayesha saw his father in him.

"I understand. I love you, mom. I gotta go out. I'll be back before dinner and I'ma get Taqiq from Jay house on the way back."

Ayesha nodded and went to pray as Lil Ali left.

Chapter Six

Cross Creek Mall

The Cross Creek Mall was the biggest mall in North Carolina with four large floors filled with designer stores, fancy restaurants, a movie theater, two food carts, a gym, race car track for go-car racing, and an arcade center with laser tag for kids.

Lil Ali and Nicole walked out of the True Religion store, holding hands and walking through the crowded mall. She wore a sunflower dress made by Louis Vuitton with sandals because it was ninety-five degrees outside. Lil Ali rocked a fitter American Eagle top with a pair of Balmain jeans with rips in the knee area, and a pair of Air Max.

"I see you getting a lot of attention today, fly girl," Lil Ali said as they walked downstairs while males and females stared at her curves and ass poking out from the side.

"Whatever, nigga, I see them niggas looking at you but anyway—as I was saying—I'm glad we get to spend time together. It be so hard with me in college and you doing your thing!" Nicole said as they walked into a Chanel store to see the latest Chanel shoes, purses, dresses, outfits and jewelry.

"I feel shit been a little crazy but you know our hearts and mind frame are in the same place," he said as she was picking up a pair of gold colored high heels and looking at the price tag that was out of her range.

"You still be in Southgates? That place been on the news every night—somebody dying or getting shot and I know Bundles your friend but he got a bad name, babe, and I just don't want you to get caught up," Nicole said, looking at some dresses, holding each one to her waist.

"I told you about that shit. Whatever choices I make will be off the strength of me. I'm my own man." Nicole sensed the seriousness in Lil Ali's tone of voice. "Okay, I know. I just worry about you," she said in her sweet country voice.

"The only thing you need to know is, I'm trying to get up in them guts," he said loud enough that an old white lady standing next to them overheard them as she looked at them, stroking her gray hair, walking away almost immediately.

"Bae, you crazy and I'm still on my cycle. Now come with me so I can try this on and are you sure my shopping spree has no limit?" she said, looking at the price tag on three Chanel dresses and some jeans.

"I told you *no limit*. I got you," he said as she gave him the funny eye, not wanting to question him in public.

"Okay, babe," she said, kissing his lips and rubbing his dick while she saw an employee staring, but she didn't care. She went into the dressing room and closed the door with the mirror attached to it, as he sat in the leather seat thinking how lucky he was to have her.

Lil Ali was turning eighteen soon, and he wanted to marry her because he was committing a sin by having sex with her and she was not legally his wife. He respected her Jewish beliefs but she wasn't really into Judaism and she knew if she would turn Muslim, her family would abandon her. He knew she was the one for him and she accepted him for him.

He looked at his new icy AP watch, realizing he had an hour and a half before their movie started, which was a romance flick starring Kevin Hart. Nicole stepped out of the dressing room in a pair of Chanel heels and dress showing her amazing physique.

"How do I look?" she said, pushing up her perfect breasts so they sat neatly in her dress then she spinned around, showing him all her ass hanging out.

"You look like a masterpiece. You're beautiful. You even look better with nothing on." He smirked, feeling his dick rise.

"Boy, you nasty. I bet you could use a quickie right now," she said, flirting, looking around to see shoppers doing their shopping and minding their business.

"I'm good on the bloody dick for now. I'll do a raincheck," he said, laughing.

"Well, I was thinking some quick head but maybe in the movie theater," she said, walking back in the dressing room to try on another outfit as he smiled like a kid with a new toy.

After she tried on a couple outfits, she was ready to check out, but she added up everything in her head and it came up to $12,350. She wanted to put some items back but he told her to chill; she was good.

Once at the counter, he paid the young white women cashier $13,000 once he saw the prices at $12,405. Before he walked out the store with a hand full of bags, Nicole pulled his arm.

"What the hell was that?" she said under her breath, wondering where he got all this money.

"You ask too many questions, let's just say I hit the jackpot. Now let's go to Wendys. Get your favorite salad and go shopping for some Gucci," he said, making her smile as they walked towards the foodcart.

***

Hours Later

Bundles had been watching T-Money's every move for the past couple of hours in a black Toyota he borrowed from one of his folk homies.

It was still daylight, so Bundles played the cut not trying to be seen and blow his cover as he posted in the far end of the front parking lot in Holly Heights.

T-Money had the skyscrapers projects, all four of the buildings, looking like the 80's and 70's in Harlem. He saw T-Money dropping off work to his workers all day in a green Range Rover with tints and peanut butter seats.

The hood was flooded with teens selling poison to their own parents and family members just to pay for the newest pair of sneakers.

The green range was pulling out the lot slowly blasting music full of goons. Bundles pulled out and headed home to go prepare for his mission tonight.

T-Money was his number one property; he only hoped Lil Ali was just as ready because he already blew most of his money in clubs ten rocks a night tricking, shopping, and he copped a new chromed out BMW.

***

T-Money was twenty-seven years old, handsome, short, loved to dress and fuck everybody babymother; he was a playboy. He been deep in the dope game for over ten years not because he wanted to, but because he had to due to his living situation. His mom was in federal prison, and so was his dad—both serving life sentences for murders and bank robberies in Mississippi when he was younger.

He grew up in Holly Heights with his aunt who was a church woman. She ended up kicking him out when she found drugs in his room. He moved in the next building with his best friend, Lavi, who was Pusha's little brother. The two started selling drugs for Pusha and never looked back.

Since Pusha was dead and Lavi was in prison for a murder, the projects was T-Money's. He was able to pay for a house in Tiffany Pines for his grandmother he took care of. She was always by his side since day one, and she knew the game in and out; she taught him a lot.

T-Money was at a BP gas station talking to Q-Rod about some money that came up short, and his capo told him he would handle it before he made their way to Club Booty Tap gentlemen club later to make it rain.

After his little meeting with Q-Rod fat ass, T-Money hopped on highway 301 and drove to his low key crib across town near Beechwood projects to pick up London and take her home. London was his main bitch that attended North Carolina State. Showty was phat, brown-skinned, boujee, sexy and classy. T-Money knew he had time to fuck the life outta her then take her home, get dressed and hit the clubs up his regular weekend.

***

Rosemary Road was a quiet middle-class neighborhood. Nothing went on in the Tiffany Pines area. Lil Ali lived a couple of blocks away while Nicole lived on the end of the block right directly across the street from the stop sign.

"Man, why the fuck did we have to come near where I live to do this shit?" Lil Ali stated, looking at the blue and white house he saw many times as a Lexus and green Range parked in the driveway.

"I ain't know his grandma lived here. You'll be okay. You don't even live on this block, and Nicole not even home. Look!" Bundles said, pointing towards Nicole's house as the black Toyota sat in a dark area near a tree.

"That's not my point but come on, let's make it quick. Stick to the plan," Lil Ali said, looking up and down the pitch-black street to see it was empty.

"Let's do it." Bundles grabbed his locksmith bag to break in the back door smoothly and disconnect the alarm system. He was the best at his work. He could get in any house with any security system.

***

T-Money had just gotten out of the shower as he dried his long dreads off, looking at the eight keys of dope he had left to his name. He had a Cuban connect who gave him the best prices and the best grade 10 dope his money could buy.

There was a Givenchy outfit laid out on the bed with two diamond-encrusted Jesus pieces and a Rolex watch worth $50,000. He began to get dressed while watching ESPN replays of tonight's game on his large flat-screen TV mounted on his wall.

His grandma would normally wake up around four to use the restroom, so the footsteps he heard made him get up but as soon as he turned around, he wished he would have never.

"Sit the fuck down, nigga," Bundles said, pointing a Draco with a knife on the barrel. T-Money sat on the floor with his shirt off and Givenchy jeans, and a double G belt above his Tom Ford boxers.

"Come on, bruh, y'all violating. Dawg, this my grandma house, ain't nothing here," T-Money said, forgetting there were eight bricks of dope on the other side of his bed.

"Oh, is that right, my nigga?" Lil Ali said, seeing him look across the room to the heating stacks of bricks. T-Money was caught red-handed. He knew the game and respected it.

"Everything is in the duffle bag in the closet. I don't want no trouble, dawg. The keys and money are all over there," he said, pointing towards his bedroom closet. Lil Ali snatched up everything, the drugs and the money, tossing it on the bed.

"Y'all look like fucking kids, man, let my grandmom live," T-Money said, trying take control of the situation until Bundles slammed the butt of the Draco in his face twice, busting his nose and lips. Lil Ali looked deeper in the closet to see a hundred designer shoe boxes. He popped the tops to see money stacks in rubber bands in three of them as he came out the closet cheesing.

Before he could even say something, shots raged out from behind him as he clocked with a spin move and sent two shots from his colt 45 with a silencer in her forehead, dropping her instantly as tears filled T-Money's eyes with rage. T-Money got up and tried to attack Bundles, but he caught three shots to the head, thanks to Lil Ali.

"Come on, grab the shit!" Lil Ali said, grabbing a couple of shoe boxes and a duffle bag as blood puddles were spilling down the stairs from T-Money's grandmother's head wound.

The two walked out the same way they came in, feeling good to be alive because the old lady with the saggy breasts almost had a clear shot.

Chapter Seven

The loud annoying sound of the alarm clock woke Lil Ali up at 5:25 a.m. as it did every morning so he could make his morning prayer before the sunrise.

He yanked his Polo bed sheet from over his face and reached towards his dresser, cutting off his alarm clock while yawning and crawling out his bed.

Luckily, Ayesha worked a double last night because he got back in late but the babysitter was asleep on the couch while Taqiq was knocked out.

Last night was a close call. Killing the old bitch wasn't in his plans, but she almost killed him and Bundles. He knew next time to be more alert.

He turned on his room lights and went to take a hot shower to wash away the fresh blood on his mind. While in the glass shower, the hot water soothed his smooth brown skin as he stood under the steamy water thinking about when he was younger and his father was alive.

Whenever he thought about his father, he felt a ball of rage in the pit of his stomach. He knew his father was murdered, as Ayesha told him, but nobody knew who did it. He wanted to find his father's killer, to let his father's name and honor rest in peace.

After washing his body three times with body wash, he made *ghusl* and *wudu* for his morning prayer. He wrapped a large towel around his navel as his chiseled body was dripping with water as he walked back into his room connected to his bedroom.

The bathroom was large with marble floors, marble sinks, a glass shower, and Bower mirrors. The ceilings were covered in fancy expensive chandeliers.

Lil Ali shut off the bathroom lights to see Taqiq in his room on his bed with his back towards him doing something sneaky.

"What I told you about sleeping in my room?" Lil Ali said, making Taqiq jump up off the bed reversely, almost dropping the 9mm pistol fully loaded in his hand. "Put that shit down!" he yelled and Taqiq tossed it on the bed as if it was a ticking bomb. He never heard his brother yell at him, so it scared him as he backed up. Lil Ali slapped him in the side of his little head, almost knocking him down.

"I thought it was a toy," Taqiq said in his low voice while rubbing his head, about to cry but he choked up before he could shed a tear.

"Never touch a gun again. What the hell is wrong with you? Do you know you could have killed yourself," Lil Ali said, picking up the loaded pistol he slept with to see if the safety was off.

"I won't, I promise, I just wanted to get you up for the Fajr prayer," Taqiq said, fixing his navy blue garment and kufi to match with a pair of Jordans on.

Lil Ali got dressed, relaxing his nerves, knowing he was slipping. He knew he should have hid his gun somewhere better because Taqiq was in his room every morning.

"It's okay but today you will write me a five-page essay on why guns are bad after school. Am I clear?" he said, looking at Taqiq's soft gray eyes.

"Man, fine," he said, crossing his little arms with an attitude because normally after school he would go play Xbox games with his neighborhood friends.

"Get ready for prayer," Lil Ali said, putting Muslim oil on his arm and on his Prada T-shirt and jeans.

"I'm ready. I was waiting for you. I'ma call the *Adhan*," Taqiq said, and proceeded to perform the Islamic call to prayer. The two lined up heel to heel as Lil Ali led the morning prayer which was two *rakats*.

After prayer they both made two big bowls of Lucky Charms cereal and laughed and talked, enjoying each other's company because Taqiq was a goofy kid—the life of the party.

"You going to clear the bowls, punk?" Taqiq asked while downing the rest of the milk in his bowl.

"Who do I look like? Mommy? Nigga, you better clean your own bowl," Lil Ali said, texting Nicole who said she was up early studying. He saw Taqiq's hair was in a ponytail and it needed to be down as well as his, so he texted Nicole asking her to do both of their hair later, and she agreed. She loved Taqiq; he was a good kid and the cutest.

"After school, Nicole is going to do your hair but this time you're not sitting between her legs. I saw your smirk last time," Lil Ali said as Taqiq smirked because he had a crush on her. The two left the crib but Lil Ali saw a note from the babysitter saying Ayesha left money for Taqiq, but he paid it no mind as he took Taqiq to school.

***

Once he dropped Taqiq, he texted his mom back as she canceled their training for today so he had time to burn, and he texted Nicole to spend some time with her.

She eagerly told him to come by her house because her mom was at work, and her pops was back home from overseas but he was on the base.

He drove to her mom's house, speeding down the highway, listening to Jon B's new album, trying to get in his groove. Tiffany Pines was close to Taqiq's school, just two exits away. Nicole lived only six blocks away from him in Tiffany Pines.

As he drove towards Nicole the back way, he saw a checkpoint with local police and military enforcement standing in the middle of the street stopping every car. When he saw why, his heart started to race. The police were placing yellow cordons around T-Money's grandma's house as police ran in and out taking notes, pictures, and searching for evidence near the driveway where a Lexus truck and Ranger was parked.

There were two cars in front of him cruising slowly as the uniformed police with assault rifles waved them on to keep moving, trying to clear the block out so the police and the forensic team looked for Dactyloscopy, fiber, finger prints, footprints, elimination prints—anything to catch the vicious gunmen.

Lil Ali stopped at a gas station to get some gas and a dozen red roses which Nicole loved, and he loved to keep her happy.

***

Minutes later he was at her doorstep to see her open the door with a big smile, looking sexy in a pair of white booty shorts showing her thick toned thighs and a tank top with no bra, showing her pierced flat stomach.

"Hi, baby, I miss you," she said, jumping in his arms as he closed her door, kissing her soft juicy thick lips to see her hair was curly and wet today.

Nicole's house was upstairs and downstairs as sky blue Farrow & Ball paint covered the walls throughout the house. The living room had wall-to-wall plush carpeting, a mini bar attached to the wall near the dining room that was worth $11,000. The custom designed marble dinner table with Jim Zivic chairs made the room look more fancy than it already was.

The two walked upstairs to her room as he passed two bedrooms; one of them was her parents' room and the other one was her mother's office because she ran a realtor company and owned a traveling agency.

Nicole's room was beautiful. It was all pink wall covering with Japanese artwork, pink carpeting, pink Ralph Pucci drapes covering her windows, a cloud platform slip-covered bed that was custom made by Ralph Lauren; with a painting of John Gotti who she talked about daily. Her room smelled like a peach candle, which was her favorite scent.

"How's school, baby?" he asked, getting comfortable on her bed, taking off his shoes as she climbed on him.

"Boy, please, you know I ace everything. I gotta take some tests for my English class. Guess what the fuck happened because I know you don't watch the news. You know Ms. Smith down the block—the old quiet lady with the Lexus truck—well, her and her son was murdered last night execution style. The whole city talking about them on social media." Nicole sat up Indian style as her phat cameltoe print poked out like a balloon.

"No wonder why they had them checkpoints. Do they know who did it?" Lil Ali asked, playing dumb.

"Nah, they still on the hunt. I heard the nigga that did it son was a big time drug dealer that had a lot of beef. I never knew she had a son. My mom so scared right now. She didn't even want to leave for work this morning," Nicole said, laying her head on his chest.

"Fuck all da, shawty, come here," he said, raising her body to his so they were face to face. The two started to kiss passionately while Lil Ali played with her wet pussy, taking off her booty shorts.

"Uhmmm, boy, you so fresh," she said, as they both undressed each other. Once they were both naked, he took the lead and made his way to her shaved phat pussy that smelled like cherries. Her pussy was pink with thin pussy lips perfectly parted into her pussy, unlike most female pussy lips that looked like roast beef.

She moaned throughout her large bedroom as he clenched her soft ass cheeks as she shook uncontrollably as he sucked the life out her pussy while her little hands ripped through her Ralph Lauren sheets. Feeling his long warm tongue made her drip intensely into her pulsating pussy as he sucked her small swollen clit like a peach.

Naked and vulnerable in his strong hold, she entangled her thick legs into the air, exposing her dripping wetness as her legs wrapped around his masculine frame as she squirmed with pleasure. His big defined arms raised her legs into her arms as he worked her dripping phat pussy like a boxer in a training session with his tongue.

She closed her eyes and enjoyed her pussy being sucked dry by the man she was in love with. The wetter his tongue game was the more her body tensed up. His head game was so official it would make a bitch kill the vice president on demand.

The only sound in the room was the slurping of sweet juices between her legs as he tasted and swallowed her sweet cum.

When he was done, she climaxed four times already. He raised up and she grabbed his large massive dick and leaned her head to his dick, and sucked it slowly. She moaned as she sucked his tip then deep-throat as much as she could, bopping her head up and down. As she left his dick coated with her saliva, his toes were curling as she went faster as she slurped until pre-cum started pouring out like a volcano every time she licked it.

"Damn!" he gritted and she looked him in his eyes while still sucking his dick as he finally cum in her mouth, shooting a big load in her mouth, then she went to spit it out as she always did. She planned to save her freaky shit for their marriage.

When she came back she saw his dick still standing tall ready for the real deal. She climbed on top of him, saddling her waist to his as his dick stretched her tight walls while she bit her bottom lip. "Fuck!" she moaned as she rode his dick in a slow grind in circles, trying take his whole length in her.

"Ugghh ohh shit, I miss you!" she screamed, going deeper on his dick. Her pussy was so tight it felt like virgin pussy as he tried to control himself from cumming as her cum soaked his thighs and her sheets, as she bounced up and down until they both cum.

They fucked for two hours straight non-stop as the smell of sweet sex could be smelled through the whole house. After the sex episode, she braided his hair then went to pick up Taqiq to do his hair and go out to eat.

Chapter Eight

Southgate

Lil Ray posted on the hood of his all-white Mercedes G-class Benz with dark tints, black rims, tan leather interior, woodgrain dash, dual screen display to the turbine, heated seats, inspired air vents, and six 12" speakers.

He was in the back of Southgate next to his aunty's place waiting on Lil Ali to come through because he finally got in touch with his high school friend.

This was Lil Ray hood born and raised; he had it on lock from the dope, crack and weed. He was a young boss at twenty. The streets raised him and his brother while their pops did prison time daily like a nine-to-five, but his pops was the main in Greensboro while his brother just came home from the feds.

Lil Ray was far from little. At six-five and two hundred and twenty pounds of lean mass, he played basketball his whole life. He even went to play point-guard for Duke University until he broke his ACL his freshman year then he turned to the streets.

Ever since his big cousin—Tootsy—gave him his first pack, he never looked back. He wasn't a killer but he had a team of assassins—Bundles and Lil Ali.

The bricks Lil Ali kept giving him for the law had him questioning his friend because he never played on this level, but he knew how he got down and lately a lot of niggas been getting robbed and bodied, and it wasn't hard for him to put two and two together. Luckily, he and Lil Ali were close since middle school, so he knew he could trust him plus he was a stand up dude.

A red Hellcat challenger came speeding through the rocky fucked up pavement as dirt trailed in the air.

"Bout time," Lil Ray mumbled, checking his big face Rolex watch. The sun was just disappearing as the humidity started to decrease, giving a warm desert heat feel. Lil Ali hopped out in all-black and gold Muslim garment looking like Malcolm X in his prime.

"What's up, dawg? You a hard fool to get in touch with!" Lil Ray approached him, embracing him.

"I'm low key, broh, you know how shit be but I'm here now. When you cope this shit, dawg?" Lil Ali said, looking at the clean white Benz parked next to the trailer.

"Sum like, cuz, but good looking for the keyz. This shit fire. The hood going crazy, my man, but check this out," he said, walking to his backseat, pulling out a gym bag full of money. "This one hundred and fifty no short," he said, handing him the bag.

"No secret, good looking, bruh, shit! I still remember you used to give me candy to sell in school," Lil Ali said, tossing the bag in his trunk, reminiscing about when he was in middle school.

"Yea, you was making me some good money," Lil Ray said, posted up watching two detectives roll by in a black Crown Vic as they did daily due to the violence in the hood.

"Shit getting ugly around here. I'm about to be out," Lil Ali said as he jumped cut boys bent the corner.

"Yea, me too but Toasty told me to tell you to meet him alone at the yellow building in an hour," Lil Ray said, reading a text from his iPhone before climbing in his Benz.

"A'ight, I think I know how he look," Lil Ali said, walking to his car, hoping police weren't waiting in the cut for him to come out to pull him off because he didn't want to get caught with $150,000.

***

Ayesha was in Golden Gym on Moccasin Road where she came to three times a week for weight training. She liked the gym. It was large, divided into sections; the bicycle area was in the back in front of the mirrors; the weight machines and free-weights were located as soon as you walked in, taking up half the gym. There was also a cardio and yoga area full of mats and medicine balls plus ab machines.

Today the gym was empty with only a couple of cops exercising there daily because the owner was a retired cop.

She wore a Under Armor top and bottoms with a pair of Nike zooms with her hair in a bun. She didn't wear her hijab when she worked out even though it was against her beliefs.

Standing in front of a roll of dumbbells, she curled two twenty-five dumbbells, almost done with her arms, shoulders, and back routine. She just so happened to look in the mirror fixing her beats headphones to see a handsome fit young man busting out of a tank top.

Seeing she only had thirty minutes left, she focused her attention back on her workout, walking towards the bicycle machines to get her last sweat. Once on the bike, she placed her iPad on the middle of the bike next to a portable digital speed motor.

Five minutes into riding and listening to the Avant album on her iPad, she saw the handsome young man approach a pull-up bar thirty feet away from her. As he was doing chin-ups, Ayesha couldn't help but see every muscle flex in his cut up sculptured back. The two made eye contact but the stare was so deep you could cut it with a knife. Ayesha caught herself and continued to paddle.

When her thirty minutes were done, she was glowing as she wiped the sweat off her face with a towel, walking to the locker room to get her purse.

She passed by muscle man and saw him staring at her and she lowered her gaze as she got up out of there. She hopped in her Audi AZ and took a deep breath, thinking about her lover—Ali—and tried to hold her emotions as she pulled off to go pick up Taqiq from the babysitter.

***

Jamel was in town watching Ayesha like a hawk, as he did whenever he came to N.C. to keep an eye on them. He even had a little apartment down here. Jamel was Ali's personal security guard. He promised Ali he would look after his family and for ten years he was sticking to that promise.

For the past month his mother had been sick with cancer so he hadn't been able to come down here from Philly to keep his promise lately. He kept a close eye on Lil Ali; he even cleaned up one of his spills in which he left a dead body behind a basketball court after an argument with another young man.

The black Nissan drove back to the airport; he was tailing Ayesha and she had her same schedule for over ten years. She still looked the same and her training skills were still amazing. He saw her training sessions and she was still lethal.

***

The Yellowbuild Club

The club was a hole-in-the-wall spot owned by Toasty and Jimmy, who owned a couple of bars around the city. *Yellowbuild* looked like a regular yellow brick building across the street from a highway and KFC. There was an upstairs and downstairs, bars on each floor, poles everywhere; strippers worked from eight to five in the morning while the club was a gambling spot during the daytime.

Lil Ali walked in the club to see red lights everywhere and a couple of customers drinking or playing with the female DJ.

"May I help you, youngin'?" an older cat with dreads and glasses asked him.

"I'm looking for Toasty," he replied as the man wiping down the bar started looking at his garment, not used to seeing Muslims around here, especially not in a known strip club. The bartender gave him a nod towards downstairs, as the dancers started to walk in to prepare for their night shift.

He made his way down the dark stairs to smell weed and pop in the air as he stopped at the front room to see over twenty niggas playing pool and shooting dice, talking shit to each other. He didn't see Toasty in sight so he made his way to the next door where he heard a nigga yelling, "I don't give a fuck when you did it. You missed, nigga, you costing me money and time. You and Rugar go handle that shit, get the fuck out my office!" Toasty yelled, shaking his head.

"A'ight," PJ said, standing to leave. He left the office, shaking his head as his diamond princess cut grill shined bright through the hallway as he ran into Lil Ali and gave him a funny look.

Lil Ali walked in the office to see Toasty leaned back in his recliner chair.

"Lil Ali, thanks for coming on short notice. Let's talk," he said as Lil Ali sat down.

Romell Tukes

Chapter Nine

Lil Ali walked in his martial art class in his white robe and black belt to see everybody bowing towards him and he returned the gesture.

The studio was small with red carpet and mats everywhere, swords posted on the wall next to Japanese handwriting everywhere. There were no chairs, sitting was considered a lazy form of a lack of ambition. The studio was up and running for fourteen years; it wasn't much, but it was the only martial arts studio in N.C.

As he walked through kids, teens, and adults, everybody yelled: "Konnichiwa" which meant *good afternoon*. Lil Ali and his mom were the main teachers; they taught Judo, Karate, and Muay Thai which was disliked by Mr. Akiyama who ran the place.

Lil Ali talked with a couple of the students as they were ready to train but he had to go speak with his teacher.

Mr. Akiyama was born and raised in Taito-Ku, Japan with his sofo (grandfather) who was nicknamed the Godfather of Kendo, which was a Japan fighting style he invented in the Imperial Palace. He arrived in America over fifty years ago with his deceased sister. Now at sixty-five he still held on to his Japanese tradition. He was only five feet with a pot belly and no hair with a gray goatee but he was fast at speed, quiet, and deadly.

Lil Ali saw a saying that read *Koru Ni*, which meant "come in".

"Hajimenoshite? (How do you do?)" Mr. Akiyama asked, smiling, sitting behind his desk reading a Japanese paper. His office was small but very clean and neat. There were two large tall bookshelves posted on the wall next to his office window. The books were all old ancient history books of Japan. He had white curtains with Japanese designs all over them, a dim light, a large fish tank with two Japanese fighting fish.

"Hai akayesama de (fine, thank you)," he replied, using the foreign language his mom taught him years ago.

"You missed two weeks but me and your mom covered you, Ali, your students need you. They all speak highly of ya," Mr. Akiyama said, looking at his photos of the snow festival in Sapper. The Japanese call Sappers Yuki Matsuri.

"I know. I'm sorry," he said, looking into his teacher's dark beany eyes that were empty.

"Are you going to college? Me and your mother talked about you. I hope you make the correct choices for your future. You have a bright future and an amazing talent. I'll hate to see it go to waste, "Akiyama stated in his low pitch voice.

"I'ma put college on hold for a while to figure things out. I want to open a bigger studio to keep kids off the streets and away from jail as well as adults," Lil Ali said with a serious face.

"Oh, I understand it takes money and time, young man, but I got faith in you. Now get to work. Your students are waiting on you," Mr. Akiyama said, smiling as he stood to leave.

***

Next Night, Greensbro

Lil Ali was solo on the mission Toasty requested for him to do alone in the Greensboro area, a small city named Highpoint where it was a hair away from the Ville.

The plan was for him to kill Toasty's Uncle—Big Ray who was Lil Ray pops. The reason was because Big Ray was stepping on his feet in Greensboro trying to take over his empire he also built out there.

Toasty ain't give a fuck if you was family or not. He didn't play games when it came to his paper, and Big Ray will find out sooner or later. He put several attempts on Big Ray's life but he managed to expect every hit. He only had one person left, and that was Lil Ali, but he knew he had to leave Bundles out of this one because he talked too much and word could get back to Lil Ray.

Big Ray wasn't the only issue he had, Jay Jay—his older son who just came home from the feds—was also trying to open up shop in one of his traps across town. Jay Jay was a known murderer but he was also a known rat. He told on a lot of good men, even Toasty's little brother—Hollow. Toasty paid Lil Ali 150k to kill both men and who was he to turn that down! He lived by the code of the street: play for keeps.

***

Lil Ali was parked at the end of the block in a gray Ford Focus sedan watching the apartment complex, where Big Ray was talking to a brown-skinned skinny nigga in his thirties.

The two were in a heated argument. Lil Ali leaned back behind the tints, checking the clock on his dashboard to see it was close to six at night, but 97 degrees. He wore a thin all-black sweatsuit with a hoodie and ski mask sitting on his head.

He was waiting for the right moment to make his move. There were too many people out and witness for him to kill a nigga in broad daylight, so he just leaned back and took a handful of popcorn, getting ready for his move.

***

Big Ray was the king in Greensboro. He was the biggest dope boy in the city, thanks to his Jamaican connect in VA. He had a big army of workers and shooters whenever needed but he was focused on his paper. He tried to teach Lil Ray and Jay Jay the game but the two didn't want to network or believe the sky's the limits in other cities like he did.

Lately violence been coming to his doorstep and he had two attempts on his life but he knew who was the cause: his nephew. He had plans for him soon but now he was focused on taking over his blocks. It was a cold game, and blood was considered water in the streets.

He just got done talking to Fat Tone, one of his workers; he owed him $80,000, and Fat Tone had been in Atlanta for two months on the Eastside getting money off his product. But Ray told him he had twenty-four hours to pay him or his goons will be at his mama crib.

Big Ray could instill fear in a nigga just with his size. He was 6'7 and three hundred pounds' solid muscle, black and ugly with dreads and a gold grill bottom and top.

***

Lil Ali saw the two tone Wraith pull off the curve with tints and rims fresh off the lot. Two hours later the black and gray Wraith pulled into a carwash on the same block of a small projects filled with kids and old people cooking out, enjoying the summer heat.

The carwash had five separated brickwalls where customers could wash their own cars, fill the tires, and take their time because it was open 24/7 hours a day.

Big Ray had both of his doors open, while he placed his mats on the ground near his supplies he used to clean out his car with as 2Pac blared through his loud system.

It was a musk dark outside due to daylight saving with only another customer cleaning his old-school Chevy cutlass caprice. Lil Ali knew it was now or never but first he had to take care of the witness.

2Pac could be heard throughout the whole lot. Lil Ali snuck behind the young driver of the Chevy and shot him in the back of his head and his body collapsed in a puddle of soap and water.

Big Ray was hopping his big head to his favorite rapper while waxing his car. As he raised his big body, he felt a long nose gun to his head but it was a silencer connected to a Glock.

"Wow, dawg—" Big Ray yelled but nobody was there as the silencer sent four shots in his head.

Southgate

Jay Jay stood in front of the Southgate entrance with Dre, Live and Foots talking shit, plotting on going out tonight to turn up. At twenty-five he looked ten years older—thanks to his five years he was stressed, which pushed his hairline back.

He had a rough prison bid getting ran up in jail to jail, stabbed four times, and almost dying twice because the niggas he ratted on was in every yard he went to. He ended up doing the rest of his time in a dropout yard in Arizona where he did three years before being released.

Now he was back getting money, selling drugs for his little brother. He hated it but his brother was the man. His father ain't fuck with him because he snitched and he knew he would do it again.

Dre sat in his dark blue with white interior leather seats sitting on 20's with TVs in every headrest, blasting an old Lil Boosie.

"Yo, what's up with Club Lite in South Cordina?" Live asked Jay Jay while he was texting a hoodrat chick from across town.

"I'm with it, bruh, you dig?" Jay Jay said with his G4 skinny frame as his long dreads covered his face.

A Ford Focus smoothly pulled up towards the crew with the window cracked enough to only see darkness in the car.

Rat-tat-tat-tat-tat-tat-tat! The sounds of the draco sounded like close range fireworks.

Jay Jay tried to run but caught two shots to the chest as well as Live while Dre pulled off getting away from the Ford Focus as fast as possible as Jay Jay and Live laid dead in puddles of dark blood under a street light.

Romell Tukes

Chapter Ten

Lil Ali patiently waited in his car looking at his dirty hood, wishing he would have washed the car before going out of town. He looked across the dark street at a nice skyscraper built with big glass windows and a glass door leading into the marble lobby. Waiting on Toasty was like waiting on your grandma to come out of bingo night.

After he did the drive by, he took the Ford Focus to Howard Park to burn it, leaving no traces. He knew Jay Jay was dead. He saw when he took his last breath before he drove off into the dark night; everything was perfect timing. He felt no type of remorse for killing Big Ray or Jay Jay rat ass. He hated rats anyway. If a man did a crime or was killing niggas but when he get caught with one goon he start telling, he was the worst coward in Lil Ali's books.

He planned to save the $150,000 or at least most of what he can and put it with the $20,550 he had left to open his mosque and studio. While thinking about his business, Toasty finally walked out the fancy building which was a block away from FSU (Fayetteville State University).

Toasty saw Lil Ali's car parked a couple of cars next to his, so he made his way to him with a big smile as his grill glowed in the dark.

"My phone ain't stop blowing up yet word is you did them niggas something unforgiving. Didn't you get rid of the car?" Toasty asked as Lil Ali climbed out his car.

"Of course but I handled my end so we even," Lil Ali said, cutting to business, not one to brag on his work.

"Tighten up, youngin, we good. I appreciate ya. Keep this between us, my nigga, you know how this shit go," Toasty said, patting Lil Ali on his shoulder before walking off. "Oh yea, I holla'd at Bundles. I gave him a new lick for both of you. It a heavy weed hit some Haitian niggas that fucking my weed flow," Toasty said as Lil Ali just nodded, climbing back in his Hellcat before taking off.

***

Today was a long day so Lil Ali planned to chill for the night. He texted Nicole while walking in his house to smell the scent of sandalwood Muslim oil in the air. He took off his sneakers to see his mom and Taqiq making the night prayer (Isha) so he rushed to make *wudu* then he joined them.

After prayer they all talked about work, school, training, and an up and coming summer trip to Disneyland for Taqiq who was overly excited about it, even though he had summer school. Once Lil Ali was done cleaning the house, Ayesha and Taqiq both went to their rooms to prepare for the night while he went in his room to take a shower and think about a location for a mosque and martial art studio.

Forty minutes later, he was in his walk-in closet filled out with shoe boxes, suits, designer jeans, shirts, coats, belts and hats he saved for years. He always stayed fly with the latest fashion. In the deep end of his closet covered by peacoats was ten assault rifles hidden behind the coats, clean with extra banana clips attached to the SK, AK, Draco and his three AR-15 straight from Russia.

He heard his phone ringing as he turned off his closet light. He saw it was Bundles, knowing he was calling to gossip or get him to come fuck some bitches with his as he always does.

"Damn, cuz, where you been? It dawg shit was fucking lite in the hood them Meadaoood fucked over Jay Jay rat ass and Live folk Lil Ray going crazy. We about to slide right now," Bundles said with a drunk slur in his voice while talking reckless on the phone.

"Damn, that's crazy, bruh, niggas is tripping. Tell him I send my regards. Dude was good people, but I ain't know Ole Bay lived, but be easy," Lil Ali said, sitting on his bed recounting the same money for the third time.

"I was calling you early today. Where was you at? Let me find out you was in some new pussy," Bundles said, laughing.

"Naw, I was with Taqiq. We went out," he said fast just so he won't try to piece some shit together.

"Oh, okay but look, Toasty put us down again on the Haitians across town but I figure we could use one more nigga for back up so I'm bringing G-Loc bruh down bad on his knuckles," Bundles said as wind could be heard through his phone in the background as if he was in a car.

"Just holla at me tomorrow," he replied before Bundles got them indicted over a phone call.

"A'ight, dawg, I love you," Bundles said as he always did when he was drunk.

"A'ight, bruh." Lil Ali hung up, shaking his head, throwing all the money in a duffle bag under the bed.

It was eleven forty p.m., so he went to check on his mom. He didn't spend a lot of time with her because of her busy work hours, but when they were training five days a week, that was the most time they spent with each other.

He walked downstairs to her room across from the kitchen and next to the downstairs bathroom.

"You okay, mom?" he asked as he saw Ayesha sitting on her bed Indian-style in her pajamas with her long hair in a ponytail, reading an Islamic book called *Understanding Knowledge*.

"Inshallah I'll always be okay, baby," she said, looking up at him. Her master bedroom was large with a walk-in closet, a fireplace, a large bookshelf, her own bathroom with a Jacuzzi which she used daily.

"We got them tournaments this coming weekend and I believe everybody is ready," he said, sitting on her Chanel bed set.

"Trust me, you're a great trainer, you're about the most skilled fighters in America, believe me," she said, proud of how far he'd come and now being able to train others.

"I know but I want to open a mosque and a martial arts studio, I know it's well needed, mom. I know Allah knows my true intention and my good deeds will outweigh the bad no matter what I gotta do to make this happen," he said, looking into his mother's bright gray eyes.

"Understood—just be smart and careful," she said as the two talked for the rest of the night like old times as he fell asleep on her bed like he used to do as a kid.

***

Next Day

Lil Ali, Bundles and G-Loc sat in his sister's trailer plotting how to get the Haitian brothers tonight as G-Loc paced the dirty carpet with all typed dog piss stains from his red-nosed pit he kept locked in the back room.

G-Loc was an eighteen-year-old high school dropout like most kids in the trailer park; he was a known shooter, that's why Bundles kept him near.

"Ayo, folk, I heard them niggas ain't nothing to fuck with, I heard they 'bout that life," G-Loc stated, taking a deep pull of granddaddy Kush.

"It's all good, folk, don't worry about them Miami niggas gangsta. I checked their resume and they not that official, dawg," Bundles said, puffing on a Newport.

"Alright. I'm down to ride, cuz," G-Loc said, feeling a little uneasy around Lil Ali; there was something about him that didn't sit right with him.

***

Lil Ray leaned the bottle of Pat Mason upside down to his thick lips, this was his way of mourning over his father and brother death. He was at Meka's crib one of his slids he been fucking since high school even though she was two years older than him.

Meka was a slim dark-skinned chick with long fake hair, nice C-cup tits, nice toned body, no ass but she had curves and a cute face, plus her swag was what attracted nigga to her; gurl was country and fly.

"You okay, baby?" she asked, watching Lil Ray drink himself to death for two days. But when she lost her brother, she recalled, she did the same shit. She climbed in the bed in a bra and panties next to him, rubbing his wide back as she heard his cries.

Chapter Eleven

Lil Ali, Bundles, and G-Loc all looked out the tint window of the long black van they stole from the YMCA an hour ago. The run-down apartment complex on All American Road had boarded windows, cracked floors and a few tenants that lived in the quiet building that was on its last leg.

The Haitian niggas owned the building but it was also one of their stash houses they thought nobody knew about.

"Dawg, it's ten thirty. I'm trying to get some pussy, cuz," G-Loc said, sitting in the driverseat dressed in all black waiting for the Haitians to arrive.

"Nigga, chill the fuck out, niggas going show," Bundles said, looking at Lil Ali who was staring at the build with a pistol in his lap.

Minutes later they saw an all-white Range Rover Sport sitting on 24 rims pull up and double park in front of the build. Lil Ali and Bundles locked at each other and smiled, knowing it was time to put in work.

***

Life was beautiful for Da-Da and his big brother—Bear. The two were from Miami, Little Haiti to be exact. Their parents were immigrants from Haiti; the slums filled with poverty and evil spirits on the small island.

Once in America, the two were forced to grow up quickly so they started selling drugs for the Cubans in Miami. Years later the brothers became Kingpins, and a big war against the Cubans broke out and caused a lot of blood in the streets which brought the feds to the city.

After the feds scooped up most of the army, the brothers were forced to shut down shop and leave town. They had been in Cordina for two and a half years with the biggest weed operation in the city.

Da-Da was tall, slim, black as midnight and handsome. At thirty years old he was very successful. Him and his brother—

Bear—ran real estate businesses, and an auto body shop in Green-ville, N.C. His brother, Bear, was the mastermind since kids. He was thirty-four years old, six-seven, three hundred and sixty pounds with long dreads covering his ugly face.

Da-Da drove fancy cars, wore a ton of jewelry and party hard while Big Bear was the opposite. Bear drove a Volvo wagon five years old and wore old no-name clothes and no jewelry to avoid federal attention. The two shared a mini mansion on the outskirts of Fayetteville to lay low and stay away from jack boys and lurkers.

Da-Da hopped out his Range, leaving the car running with his new joint, Jasmine—a thick sexy redbone who had a phat ass, big titties, and thick curves but she was barely legal. She told Da-Da in the club last week she was twenty but she just turned seventeen two days ago. She already sucked his dick and she let him finger her tight young pussy, but she planned to let him fuck tonight and he promised her a Birkin bag.

Da-Da told her he'll be back. He had to drop some money off as he hopped out with a gym bag full of money. He bopped his way into the run-down building with his swag on a million thinking about how good her head game was, and he knew the pussy was even better.

He rocked a all-white Versace suit with a Jesus piece swinging from his neck as his shoulder-length dread bounced with every step, as he walked into his building.

***

Jasmine had Lil Wayne album *Carter V* knocking in the car with the windows down, thinking about how she was going to ride Da-Da dick so good he might buy her two Birkin bags and some Gucci, Lovy, Fendi, and Prada.

She was so busy singing Lil Wayne she didn't see Lil Ali appear at the window until he startled her. "You scared the fuck outta me," she said, holding her chest while looking at the young man in front of her who was dressed in all black and sexy as hell.

"I ain't mean to scare you," Lil Ali said softly while she turned down the music. Jasmine looked to the build to see if Da-Da was coming out. The nigga was cute at the window but he wasn't worth her designer bag.

"You just gonna stand there or ask for my number?" Jasmine said, starting to feel uneasy by his awkward approach.

Lil Ali swiftly swung a long thin blade across her neck, slicing her throat open like a zipper as blood squirted on the dashboard and windows. Leaving her dead as blood soaked her green tight dress she boosted from Nordstrom yesterday.

***

Da-Da stepped out his build with his head down as the night humidity dropped from earlier. He had a lit blunt filled with blueberry Kush dangling from his lips as he walked back to his Range feeling his dick harden just thinking about what he wanted to do to Jasmine when they got to the motel. He promised her a designer bag but he knew that wasn't going to happen because after he fucked her, he planned to drop her off and block her number.

"What—the—fuck—" Da-Da screamed like a bitch as he saw blood all over his truck as Jasmine's head was leaned to her far left as if it was about to roll off. Before he could turn to run or even pull out his pistol, he felt a sharp pain to his head as everything in sight went pitch black.

***

Da-Da woke up twenty minutes later in wet grass tied up like a prisoner with thick rope to see three niggas standing in front of him.

"What the fuck going on, man? I swear I didn't even fuck shawty. I don't even know that bitch," Da-Da stated, thinking one of these niggas was her babyfather because this wasn't his first time fucking with other niggas' bitches or babymothers.

"Nigga, shut the fuck up. This a stick up!" Bundles said, aiming his AK-47 with a knife on the end.

"Yea, nigga," G-Loc said, jumping around like a kid hyping himself up, as Lil Ali shook his head, ready to get down to business.

The crew was near a small lake behind Southgate where niggas would bring bitches to where they ran trains on nasty freak bitches in the hood.

"Listen, let's make this easy on all of us. Call your brother, tell him we want $225,000 in cash and fifty pounds of weed, no mid, no funny shit, no cops, and he got forty-five minutes or ya dead!" Lil Ali said in a calm tone as if he was talking with a priest about a confession.

"Okay, understood," Da-Da said as he had a headache from the huge lump he had in the back of his head. Lil Ali placed his phone he took from him to his ear as Bear's phone was ringing.

"Hello," a deep sleepy voice answered the phone.

"Bro, they got me and they not playing. They want 50 pies and 225k—"

"What! Nigga, we got you and I told your dumb ass!" Bear said, cutting him off, angry. Bundles snatched the phone from Lil Ali.

"Look, nigga, you got forty minutes to get to Southgate with that or your brother dead and you dead when we catch you!" Bundles yelled into the phone.

"Okay, bruh, chill, I'm coming right now. I knew how this shit go, bruh, I'll call you when I get there," Bear said, hanging up.

"Done, nigga!" Bundles said, handing him the phone. "Me and G-Loc going wait on this nigga just in case he pull some funny shit, folk," Bundles said, walking off.

"I'll pay you triple if you let me leave, homie, please!" Da-Da begged with tears in his eyes, trying to escape this death trap. "I gave my life to Jesus," he said.

"Nigga, shut your bitch ass up. Let's see if Jesus save you from this," Lil Ali said, shutting him up.

***

Bear drove into Southgate in an all-black Cadillac Escalade truck with rims, in deep thought, wondering who kidnapped his little brother. Over the years they made so many enemies he had no clue who would kidnap Da-Da, but he planned to get to the bottom of it.

As he drove down Stiss Round, which was dark with no street lights, he saw a van flashing its headlights at him parked on the side of the road, as he pulled over.

He hopped out to see two teenagers walking his way. He thought it was a joke but he knew young niggas around this way was just as dangerous as an older nigga.

"Where it at?" Bundles asked with his assault rifle dangling from his neck on a shoulder strap as G-Loc had his draw aimed at the big black nigga.

"It's all in the trunk and backseat but where is my brother?" Bear demanded off jump, not trying to give something to get nothing.

"Nigga, fall back, we'll get to that in a second," Bundles said, nodding towards G-Loc so he can make sure Bear played fair.

"It's all here," G Loc said, smiling.

"Walk. I'ma take you to your weak ass brother," Bundles said as he aimed his gun at Bear, telling him to walk through the woods in a thin dirt trail path.

Once in the deep wet field, Bear saw Da-Da tied up on the floor with a lumped up head so big it looked like he was having an allergic reaction.

"Etes vous feu"? Bear asked Da-Da with an evil look, questioning his gangsta as a man and killer.

"Enough of that French shit. Yo, Bundles, we good?" Lil Ali said, cutting his eyes at Bundles.

"Yea, we good, homie," G-Loc answered for him.

"A'ight," Lil Ali said, shooting Da-Da in his face three times. Bear rushed the closest nigga to him which was Bundles. He tried to snatch his AK but he was putting up a fight as G-Loc was just standing there watching.

"*Boom! Boom!* Lil Ali shot Bear in the side of his head, dropping him as his body collapsed on top of Bundles.

"Get rid of the van," Lil Ali camly told G-Loc as he took off, Bundles ice grilled G-Loc for not helping him.

"That nigga almost killed me, folk, and that nigga standing there watching on some bitch ass shit!" Bundles said, catching his breath.

"Nigga, just get your weight up. Come on, let's get this shit and we gotta get rid of dude's car then we split the diner," Lil Ali said, walking through the dark trail that led to the streets.

Chapter Twelve

Bundles was on his way to meet a slim chick he met at the club the other night.

The slim dark-skinned chick lived near Meadowood, a section he hated to even drive past because Southgate and Meadowood had a strong dislike for each other for years.

His Impala stopped at the far way directly across the street from the flat housed projects full of young niggas outside smoking and blasting music from niggas' cars. Bundles turned up his sound system as Pastor Tray filled his trunk as niggas looked towards the reek to see where the loud music was coming from, knocking their system out the picture.

Bloc! Bloc! Bloc! Bloc! Boom! Boom! Bloc! Bullets riddled Bundles' driver and passenger windows as well as his car door as he peeled off on the green light, almost hitting two cars on the other side of the street.

"Fuck!" Bundles screamed in pain as he felt a sharp pain rip through his shoulder as he saw four niggas in his rearview still busting at his car until he busted a sharp left. He was five minutes away from the hospital but he knew the police would be on his ass so he drove to his aunty's house who was a licensed nurse. He turned his music back up, laughing, thinking about revenge on the whole hood. He knew they fucked up missing an attempt on his life; he found it funny.

***

Toasty pulled into the lower garage of his apartment complex in his Porsche, tired from his trip. He just came back from opening a new trap house in Winston-Salem with two dyke chicks he sold bricks to for years.

His apartment building was all fancy condos for middle or upper class people. He was the only person of color in the tall cobblestone sky-rise build. He walked through the polished tiled floor to the elevator to the sixth floor where he lived.

As soon as his dick started to get hard thinking about Oliva's toned, smooth, fresh scent body, he heard a male voice as the lights flicked on to see Lil Ray aiming a big 50 cal pistol at him with a silencer and a beam on it.

"You think you got all the sense, you let greed and thirst take over you and that led you to kill my pops. I ain't really give a fuck about Jay Jay. He was a rat just like I always knew you was a bitch scared to put in work yourself," Lil Ray said, dressed in a hoodie and sweatpants with a crazy look as the odor of Hennessy could be smelled on his breath.

"Nigga, I made you and your pops. This game is called chess, not checkers, little nigga, and I make move to win the game so don't it personally. Sometimes a nigga Queen gets eliminated!" Toasty stated, ready to die because he knew Lil Ray wasn't going to let him walk. He cursed himself every second for leaving his pistol in his car.

"Nah, dawg, you got it fucked up. My family isn't a board game but I do respect law," Lil Ray said, lifting the cannon.

"Hold on, bruh—wait, cuz, listen—" *Psst! Psst!* Bullets pierced Toasty's skull as it took two seconds for his dead body to fall on his tan European carpet. Lil Ray stepped over the puddle of blood, still tipsy from earlier, thinking of his next move.

***

Days Later

Lil Ali was laying low after the two bodies of Da-Da and Bear were found. It was a big thing in the news and in the hood. For almost two weeks he was chilling at home and at the martial art studio preparing his fighters for the state competition.

With Bundles still healing from his injury and the recent news of Toasty's death, his robbing career was on hold. When he heard about Toasty's death, all types of thoughts went through his head. It could have been a revenge plot for the death of Pusha, T-Money, or the Haitian niggas. Anything could have been the cause of his death and he wasn't trying to take no chances.

***

The red Hellcat was speeding down the highway doing eighty miles per hour on his way to Nicole's campus to spend some time with her.

He'd been busy with training and Nicole been so busy with school; the two haven't been able to spend time with each other. Since Nicole's roommate was in Ohio for the weekend, he decided to come see her; plus, she was talking freaky and he was trying to see if she was just talk.

Once on the FSU campus, it was like party central around eleven at night: everybody was yelling, screaming drunk, playing loud music, couples were cuddled up on the grass, and students were carrying their drunk friends back to their dorms because they were too drunk to walk. Lil Ali always fit in because he looked like a running back or quarterback, plus he was fine as hell so all the students were on him, thinking he was a new freshman everytime.

He made it to her dorm with a box in his hand with a red bow. The box contained a $15,000 bracelet he bought from Tiffany's jewelry store this morning. As he walked through outside, the walkway was filled with party goers. He knocked on Nicole's door to see a party going on across from her. All the dorms were located outside in the open, so parties and loud music was acceptable among the administration.

"Damn, gurl, who dat? He is fine as fuck. I'll fuck the shit outta him," a Spanish chick told two black chicks as they stood outside the apartment smoking cigarettes as music could be heard from inside their apartment.

"I think that's Nicole man. I hate her stuck up ass," one of the chubby black girls said as Nicole opened her door in a Dolce & Gabbana tank top and booty shorts with a little make-up on looking sexy with her matching manicure toes and nails.

"Hi, baby," she said loudly so the bitches could hear as she kissed his soft lips while ice grilling the thots known as shores across from her before slamming the door in their nosey ass faces.

"I got something for you," he said, walking into the clean living room. The apartment was small but nice with white and black wallpaper, a large flat screen in the living room, white carpeting, black leather couches, two bedrooms, two bathrooms, a small kitchen and a study area in the far corner of the living room.

"Them hoes say anything to you?" she said with her arms crossed with a frown.

"What? Nicole, don't play with me. I would never disrespect you like that," he said, grabbing her soft ass cheeks, smelling her Prada perfume for women.

"I know," she said, knowing he was a really good boyfriend.

"Here," he said, pulling out a Tiffany box as her eye budged open as she opened it to see a diamond bracelet.

"Oh my god! Thank you, baby, this is so nice!" she shouted, jumping in his strong muscular arms.

She grabbed his hand, led him to her room near the kitchen. Her room had photos of him everywhere and 50 Cent, her favorite rapper. They both quickly undressed, admiring each other's perfect bodies.

Nicole laid on her queen-size bed, shoving her teddy bears on the floor and was naked as she spread her legs wide, showing her clean shaved pink pussy.

Lil Ali's dick was hard at the sight of her as he climbed between her legs, rubbing his tip against her wet pussy. He slowly slid his dick in her tight walls, trying to loosen her up because her pussy was naturally tight.

"Uhmmm, uggh-h-h!" she moaned deeply while digging her nails into his back muscles. Minutes later he was deep in her guts, tearing her pussy up.

"Uggh fu-c-c-k me!" she yelled as she felt herself about to cum.

"Oh, I'm cumming!" she yelled as he was long stroking her while sucking on her light brown hard nipples. When she cum, it squirted it like a waterfall as he pulled out while her cum splashed everywhere. She was still squirting as she grabbed his dick and started sucking it while playing with her clit with her free hand as her bed got soaked.

"Uhmm, baby, damn!" he moaned as she deep-throated his whole piece as his eyes rolled in the back of his head as he shot a load in her mouth, as he continued to suck while letting it all drip out her mouth.

He put her on all fours as she bounced her ass up and down, entering her from behind as she moaned softly. Within seconds he had her running from the dick as her waist thrust into his hips with a force back and forth.

"Oh-h-h shit! I'm bout to come ag-ai-n," she yelled as she threw her ass back harder on his dick, trying to take it all. When she came, he came in her at the same time as cum was pouring from her vagina.

"Lift me up and fuck me," she said, smiling as she jumped up. Lil Ali did as he was told. He fucked her on the wall for twenty minutes, then they made the way to the living room and fucked all over the place for hours.

Nicole even fucked him in her roommate's room on her bed, dresser, and floor.

After four hours of sex, they were both sore, sweaty, tired and ready to cuddle. He ended up spending the night and woke up to some of the best head he had in his life so far and breakfast in bed.

Romell Tukes

Chapter Thirteen

Womack Hospital

"Hey, Ayesha, how's the kids? I saw Taqiq at summer school the other day when I dropped off Hannana. They are in the same class," her co-worker—Emma—said as she walked into the X-ray room where Ayesha was looking over some CAT scans for one of the doctors.

She stopped and looked at Emma who sat directly next to her as she always did because she was an up close individual. Emma was a beautiful white woman with long blond hair, blue sparkle eyes, nice full lips, and a beautiful smile. At thirty-six she took good care of her toned body; she was constantly in the gym. She had an eight-year-old daughter turning nine this coming Tuesday.

"The kids are great. Ali working at the center preparing for college and Taqiq doing good in summer school. What more could a mother ask for?" she replied, reading the small TV monitor showing broken ribs and a shift spine.

"Great. Um, guess what! You remember the dark butter pecan guy I told you I met two week ago?" Emma asked, seeing her blank expression. "Well, you may not, but anyway we went on a date and—Oh my gosh!—the worst ever. It was a total mess. He had no manners, a lack of respect for people at the restaurant. Gurl, I had to cut it short," Emma said, shaking her head.

Ayesha knew Emma loved black guys. She even had a baby by one who is currently serving a twenty-year sentence in prison for a robbery and attempt murder.

"You sure know how to pick them but at least you had a date," Ayesha said with a chuckle as Emma just looked at her because she had no clue how a woman so beautiful, smart, and educated can be single and a single mother just as herself.

"Shit! I wish I still looked eighteen yang. I don't know how you do it. Botox couldn't even save me. You should see the way all these guys look at you even when you wear ya hijab. You can't hide your beauty. I think the odds are against me because I'm white but I just

95

love me some chocolate drops," Emma said as both women laughed.

"I gotta go to the third floor station. I'll be back," Ayesha said, getting up with a folder in her hand as she left the room.

***

At night time the hospital was quiet especially after visiting hours at nine p.m. but the emergency room and the labor and delivery floor was always busy with traffic at all hours of the night.

Ayesha walked down the long narrow marble hallways looking at photos of doctors, employees of the month, charity funders, and patients who beat diseases such as cancer all hanging on the walls throughout the bright hallway.

Texting Lil Ali as she got on the elevator alone was something she did throughout the night; she was always concerned about their safety.

She texted him goodnight and she was pulling a double. He replied *OK*, adding that Nicole was coming over.

She said, "Okay, make sure Taqiq get to school on time and go to bed early." She liked Nicole because she was smart, mature, beautiful, and a good girl with a career ahead of her self. She only wished she was a Muslim woman for her son but she couldn't force religion upon her. She only hoped she'll make the right choice before it's too late.

Once on the 3rd floor, she saw Dr. Wein Liv standing by the station on the phone. The 3rd floor was a little chilly and had a strong odor of wet paint from the fresh paint in the lobby restrooms.

After the doctor got off the phone, she handed him the folder of the patient CAT scans he asked her to review. She explained to him what was wrong and what needed to be done to prevent further injury. The doctor wrote down every word she said and went to prescribe his patient meds.

The station was empty as always. It was small with two chairs, two computers, a small file cabinet, and a fax machine attached to the printer.

Ayesha logged in on the computer to catch up on her work.

"Excuse me, Ms," a male voice said that startled her a little as she looked up to see a familiar face.

"How may I help you?" she said, trying to refrain from too much eye contact. She saw it was still twenty minutes before visiting hours were over

"I'm looking for Ms. Chestnut," the handsome man said, remembering her from the gym because of her hijab. It was hard to really tell but her eyes and skin complexion was one in a million.

"Oh yes, Ms. Chestnut is in room two-ten," she said, knowing the nice woman who was on her deathbed because of brain cancer; she'd just come out of a coma.

"Thank you. I'll be short. I know visiting hours are almost over. I been on the base all day fresh from Iraq," he stated.

"Yes, I understand you're okay," she said, looking at his army uniform that hugged his muscular body tightly.

"I saw you in the gym the other week?" he asked as she tried to hide her blush.

"I believe so, your mother is so sweet she tells all the nurses about you," Ayesha said as he chuckled.

"Y'all have to forgive but I'm Jamel, your name is?" he asked, not wanting to be rude.

"Where is my manners! I'm Ayesha," she said, embarrassed.

"Before I go—I was wondering if we can get a cup of coffee one day when you're free. With all due respect I know you're a Muslim woman. I took Islamic studies in Germany while in college," he said.

"Uhmm, I don't normally do this but why not take my number?" she said, writing it down for him.

After a couple of seconds of talking, Jamel went to spend the rest of his minutes with his mom who was given seventy-two hours left to live. This was his reason for being able to leave Iraq on an emergency notice. General Chestnut had been in the Marines twelve years since he was eighteen. Now at thirty-four he had rank, money, no kids, and no family except a dying mother.

***

Club Booty Tap

Bundles posted up in the strip club VIP section with a couple of his goons showing off with six bottles of Ace in two ice buckets and bottles of Moet and Chandon Rose everywhere.

The strip club was a hole-in-the-wall spot with one bar, one pole, a small stage with mirror surround. There was a stage as well as a DJ booth that could only hold one person.

The strippers weren't the best in the city; some had stretch marks everywhere, odors, bullet hole wounds, prison tattoos on their ass but they all got ass naked.

There were five strippers twerking in front of the gang of young men in the dim VIP as money was all over the floor.

Bundles sipped from his baby bottle full of lean, feeling tipsy as a dark-skinned thick bitch was grinding on his dick to a "2 Live Crew" song.

Lately, shit was getting crazy in Southgate; they were warring with the whole city, niggas was having shoot-outs at the Frisk Movie Theater, the mall parking lot, Wendys drive-through. A Southgate nigga was shot to death with his four-year-old son. There was even a shoot-out in front of the police station the other day and both gunmen were arrested on the scene.

The news media been having a field day and that brought the feds into town, so Bundles was laying low in an apartment on the outskirt of the Villie. He was cooped up in his apartment for weeks while his goons controlled the crime violence in the hood.

He still kept in touch with Lil Ali. When he spoke to him earlier, he was at some fighting tournament in Greenville.

While his dick was standing at attention, his vision was starting to blur as his shooters next to him were all turned up and tossing money as G-Loc was standing on the leather couch pouring liquor on the dancers as they enjoyed it.

The dancer in Bundles' lap felt his third leg and whispered in his ear: "For the right price I can make that big dick touch the back of my throat."

Bundles heard every word she said as he slowly bopped his head to the Gucci Mane lyrics. He still had $100,000 left from all his savings plus the lick he and G-Loc did in S.C. two days ago in Columbus where they robbed a mid level drug dealer for sixty grand.

He tapped Lil Mafia on his shoulder to let him know he was about to slide to the restroom for some head. Lil Mafia was so busy playing with a stripper's tight dripping wet pussy he didn't hear one word Bundles said as he yelled right over the bad music.

Before he could even stand, he tried to get a balance as the dancer helped, as her long saggy breasts swagged with every motion.

"FBI—FBI—FBI—FBI—Freeze!"

The feds busted in from every angle as some were already in the club acting as civilians. They ran straight to the VIP section

"Fuck!" Bundles shouted, seeing the chaos going on as feds was rushing the spot with assault rifles.

Lil Mafia was so high off molly and wet he thought it was a hit, so he pushed the red bone skinny dancer on the floor and pulled out a 380 special.

Boom! Boom! Boom! Boom! echoed from his pistol until the feds riddled his body with forty-seven shots as his frail body fell on his cousin's lap, and everyone else surrendered after they saw Lil Mafia's blood all over the VIP section as the dancers were still screaming.

***

The feds got the men they were looking for—Bundles and G-Loc—for two murders and they also got a couple of niggas on gun charges while the rest they let go outside after rounding everyone up.

Once in the interrogation room, Bundles sat in the cold room that smelled like cigarette ashes and piss.

"You know you fucked up. If you haven't been watching the news, I am up to date, you fucking dummy. You and your buddy killed the Chief of Police's son during a drive-by last month in Meadowood. The kid was visiting his girlfriend and caught a stray bullet with another teenager," the agent said, staring him down while unbuttoning his blazer and tie. The agent was a white man in his mid-forties, fit, gray hair, and a shitty attention. Agent Frazier was a professional in breaking down criminals within seconds. That's why he was in the room.

"That wasn't me, dawg, I swear on my mama I never pulled the trigger but I saw who did. I was only the driver when dude hopped out busting like a maniac. I'm telling you that shit was fucked up," Bundles said with a serious fearful look.

"What was the person wearing and what kind of car y'all was driving?" Agent Frazier asked, taking notes, not knowing it was going to be this easy as he gave Bundles a mischievous grin.

"A Nike tracksuit and we drove a Nissan Maximum all gray—I believe it's two years old," Bundles said as the agent looked in the mirror and gave his co-workers on the other side of the double mirror thumbs up.

"So he killed the two kids?" the agent asked.

"Yes, sir," Bundles stated with confidence.

"Oh yeah, I forgot you're being charged with another murder—to correct myself—a double murder of Larry Boner aka Pusha and his girlfriend Ebony Harbisan," the agent said, sliding him another murder indictment with two counts.

Bundles cried like never before as he started telling everything from his childhood to everytime he took a shit and piss in his life.

Chapter Fourteen

Lil Ali sat on the hood of his car enjoying the breeze from the river as the cloud penetrated the city, letting off a morning breeze. The wind chills were only at ten miles per hour as the morning sun laid between the clouds.

This was his place of relaxation to clear his mind and thought process whenever he had too much shit on his mind. Since Bundles' arrest for the murders, he been laying low just in case his name was in the indictiment, but the case was posted all over the news so he figured he was good.

There was no doubt in his mind that Bundles would hold it down like the true G he was, but he didn't really know G-Loc. He knew he only had one option, and that was to get rid of G-Loc before he became a federal witness.

Lil Ali stared off into the crystal clear water, thinking about another issue at hand which was Lil Ray because since Toasty's death, he'd been acting very weird. He knew Lil Ray had something to do with Toasty's death. He only hoped he kept his mouth closed.

Checking his watch, he knew it was the perfect time to go check Lil Ray's temperature to see if he got any funny vibes. Taqiq was at school, so he had at least five hours before it was time to go pick his brother from summer school.

He hopped in his Hellcat, pulling out the empty parking to only see ducks swimming around and park employees cleaning the playground area. He knew Lil Ray's schedule like the back of his hand since the death of his pops and brother.

***

Lil Ray walked out the liquor store on the corner across the street from Southgate. It was ten in the morning, so he caught the store as soon as it opened. Normally, hoodlums would be surrounding the store shooting dice and slanging dope, but today the block was quiet and empty.

He recently ran outta work so tonight he had to go outta town to re-op on some pure coke from his Dominican connect in Atlanta.

Lately, the hood been on fire—police raids, fed raids, and niggas from the other side been shooting up the hood almost everynight.

Since last night, he been posted up in Wilson trailer with a dope fiend who normally cooked coke for him; he was the best chef in the hood.

Being under so much stress caused him to drink and lose focus on the paper chase especially after burying his pops and brother two days ago.

Lil Ray pulled up to the trap in his all-white Toyota Corolla to see Lil Ali's Hellcat pulling up from the opposite way.

"What's good, big dawg?" Lil Ali said, embracing Lil Ray who gave him an awkward look as if he was trying to read him.

"Nothing, fool, just laying low shit cuz I saw Bundles and G-Loc all over the news. I thought you would have been jammed up too." Lil Ray was carrying two croc bottles into a small trailer near the back end of the large trailer park.

"Nah, bruh, I'm a little smarter than that but those are the guys," Lil Ali said, following him inside the trailer to see a crack head sleeping on the dirt couch. The trailer smelled like piss and crack with beer cans and empty liquor bottles everywhere.

"Come to the back, I been meaning to scream at you anyway," Lil Ray yelled over the TV as Jerry Springer blared through the small trailer.

Once in the back, Lil Ali was stepping over clothes, garbage, roaches, old food and old used condoms. He never knew how niggas could live like this, and this was considered a traphouse.

"I got a question, did you have something to do with—" he paused and turned around when he heard the sound of a gun click.

"I knew you wasn't as dumb as you look, bruh, but to answer your question—yeah, I killed your brother and father but it's only business, nothing personal. I'm sure you understand," Lil Ali stated as tears rolled down the big man's face.

Lil Ray stared at the colt 45 with anger and hate because he trusted Lil Ali. He never thought he would cross him outta all people; he wouldn't believe him.

"Don't look so surprised, my guy, it's no such thing as a friendship in the jungle. Why do you think tigers got stripes? I'll answer that for you—to let niggas know to stay the fuck away. I did you a favor, bro, your brother was a rat and your pops rather feed a random petty nigga than put his own sons on," Lil Ali stated as Lil Ray's face wrinkled with anger as he rushed him at full force.

Lil Ali sidestepped the giant and kicked him in his jaw, breaking it as his body landed on a pile of clothes.

Boom! Boom! Boom! The shot sounded like thunder as Lil Ray's head looked like a bowling ball as blood poured out his head like a river.

Lil Ali saw a duffle bag sticking out from under the small twin size bed with no sheets, and piss stains all over it. He snatched the bag to see it was open and full of blue faces which made him smile as he proceeded to exit the room, only to see Wilson staring at him and the pistol in his hand. Wilson was frail, old, dirty, no teeth left in his mouth, so he only ate soft food, and his skin was pale and ashen from days of not showering.

Before he said a word, a female quickly emerged from the bathroom wearing a pair of faded jeans and a Fubu T-shirt with holes. She was in her late forties, with small saggy breasts, no ass, a long neck and thick lips she used to get what she needed. She was here to suck Lil Ray's dick for crack as she has been doing since he started selling. Mya had the best head game or at least she was considered in the top five. She could deep throat a pole with ease.

Mya had a crack pipe in her hand, ready to share a hit with Wilson. The room was silent as the fiend stared at the pistol in his hand.

"Well, I see you later," Mya told Wilson as she grabbed her purse nervously as Wilson gave her a nasty look as she tried to rush for the door until she caught two bullets to the dome.

When Wilson saw her body drop like a bag of rocks, he closed his eyes and gripped his crackpipe so tight it almost broke as Lil Ali filled his chest with bullets, leaving him dead with his pipe still in his bear grip.

Romell Tukes

Chapter Fifteen

It was midnight as the red Hellcat slowly creeped on the dead end block parking behind a Dodge minivan. He looked at the yellow and blue two-story house with its lights on as he killed his ignition.

Lil Ali screwed his silencer on his German ruger he has yet to use but tonight was the night he planned to use it on G-Loc who was hiding out in the house across the dark street. He'd been on G-Loc tail for a couple of days and he knew he would be getting outta town soon because he brought the same greyhound tickets earlier.

Not trying to wait any longer, he looked up and down the dark block for any witnesses as he tied his hoodie tightly. He knew with G-Loc being free, Bundles' life was finished and maybe his if he didn't do this before it was too late.

***

"Nigga, you need to get the fuck off my coach and sell some of them damn pounds of weed you got stanking up my damn crib," Cheryl said, standing in her living room, blocking her TV with one hand on her slim hips.

Cheryl was G-Loc's older sister, pretty and independent. At five-one her frame was perfect, small breasts, nice round ass with a little cuff and smooth brown skin. She stood in front of him wearing tights and a Nike tank top fresh out the gym. Her pussy was stuffed between her thongs, spreading her pussy lips apart as it looked like two fists.

"Chill, cuz, I told you I'ma have some money for you before I leave. You know I can't be out there selling drugs. I'm still trying to lay low. You know my fucking situation," he said, kicking her legs so she could get out his way of the TV.

G-Loc was happy to be free but he had to sell his soul for his freedom. He ratted on Bundles and Lil Ali plus a couple of drug dealers from Southgate who was fucking his babymother. He was planning hopping on the Greyhound in the morning going to Texas to chill with his cousin—Pun— who was clocking major paper.

"Nigga, fuck outta here. You put yourself in that shit letting niggas use you, dummy, look at daddy still in prison never coming. You need to get your shit together and get your foot off my damn table," she said, walking off as the doorbell rang.

"Yea, whatever, bitch," he mumbled under his breath as she went to answer the front door wondering if it was her best friend Simone who he wanted to fuck. She was black, Japanese, and Korean. She was out of his class but that ain't stop him from trying every time her thick ass came around. Seconds later he heard lite sniffles as if someone was crying. When he backed back, he almost shitted himself as he jumped up in a nervous reaction as he saw Lil Ali pointing a pistol to the back of his sister's head as she walked back inside the living room.

Lil Ali shot him twice in his thighs and he fell on the wooden tiles crying in pain, trying to stop the blood but it was useless.

"Move again—the next shot is your head," Lil Ali said as he told Cheryl to get her skinny ass on the floor with him, and she did as she was told.

"I told you, George, you should have never did that shit!" Cheryl yelled through her crying, referring to him snitching.

"So I guess I don't even have to ask George, uhh—" Lil Ali said, knowing his name was in the mix of the murders.

"Man, I'm sorry, dawg, I had to save myself. They told me I was facing life but they don't have nothing on you besides my statements," G-Loc said as if that was making it any better.

"Thanks for the heads-up, bitch ass nigga!" Lil Ali then fired five bullets into his heart and shot Cheryl in her head, leaving both of them in a swimming pool dark red with blood.

***

Cumberland Jail

Bundles was called downstairs for a legal visit from his unit which was a dorm that held eighty men; it was the belly of the beast.

Once in the empty visiting room full of square tables and plastic chairs for family and friends to sit in, he made his way to the back near the snack machine across from room three.

He saw two cops dressed in suits awaiting him with his lawyer—Mr. Napoleon—who was pacing back and forth nervously. He sat down, straightening his prison uniform without greeting nobody in the room.

"Obviously it doesn't matter who we are. It only matters why we're here present with your lawyer," the Japanese detective stated as Bundles leaned back in his chair with his arms crossed, mean mugging.

"Ya cc-defendant was brutally murdered last night as well as his sister and we believe you had something to do with that. Maybe he knew something ya was scared of and didn't want it to come to light. Either way, you're fucked. Conspiracy to murder isn't nothing nice especially with what you got going on already," the other detective said, drinking a sip of starbucks coffee with his yang blue eyes fixed on his lawyer who stood there silently.

"What the fuck you talking about, dawg? I been in prison, I ain't got nothing to do with that. I swear on everything, bruh," Bundles shouted, pissed off.

"I'm sure you had probable cause," the Japanese cop said sharply with a grin.

"Cracker, are y'all stupid! I had nothing to do with that. Napoleon, you just going let these niggas railroad a nigga?" he said, looking at his lawyer who made no eye contact.

"Look, kid, help us help you. Do you have a clue who did it? Give us something. You already got a lot on your plate," the young rookie detective cop said.

"Help them," Mr. Napoleon finally opened his mouth.

Bundles thought hard. *Who could have taken G-Loc out the game?* Then it hit him like a ton of bricks from the sky.

"If I tell you, I'ma need Witness Protection for me and my family," Bundles said seriously, staring at the white ceilings.

"Granted, kid," the rookie detective said quickly as if it was already in the process as he started the type recorder and began to write in his yellow notebook.

"His name is Ali Jr., but people call him Lil Ali," Bundles said with a long pause, taking a deep beath as he told them about Lil Ali's vicious murders and how he knew he was the one responsible for G-Loc's murder. This was his first time snitching on Ali. He gave the feds enough info to get them off his back but he just told the two cops everything.

***

Ayesha looked over at her young handsome son dressed in his gray Muslim garment. He was looking out her tint windows as his mom drove him to school since she was off today.

"Did you complete your work assignment for Ms. Pearl class?" Ayesha asked as she drove through the morning traffic with her sunroof open, enjoying the summer morning breeze.

"She wants us to turn it in tomorrow but I did it last night. Ali helped me with the big bang theory," he said, looking at her

"Okay, how do you like summer school?" she asked.

"I'd rather be at camp," he said as she pulled up in front of the school behind a bus and a couple of cars dropping their kids off. Ayesha didn't want him at summer camp. She knew in summer school he could learn more.

"You'll be good. See you later," she said, kissing his cheeks.

"Ucckk!" he said, wiping her kiss. "Mom. I'm too old for that," he said, climbing out the Audi. "I love ya," he said, walking inside the cobblestone castle building with other kids.

Ayesha laughed as she pulled off to see a black and white work van full of Mexicans about to go to work somewhere but they had all suspicious looks on their faces. She drove by, not looking too obvious, not trying to attract any attention. She drove to the gym thinking she was getting extremely paranoid.

Hours Later

Lil Ali pushed his car down the packed traffic jam on the highway, going to pick up his little brother from school because it was a half day but the families got a late notice.

He just left Nicole's house when his mom called him from home telling him to go pick Taqiq up from summer school before noon. Minutes later, he was getting off the exit leading to Taqiq school, he had his windows down blasting a Rick Ross album.

***

Taqiq stood in front of the school with a gang of kids and teachers waiting on parents to pick up their children from their half of day. Taqiq looked down the street looking for his mom's Audi but only saw a black and white van slowly approaching them.

"Ricky, I think this is your uncle," one of the teachers said to the only Mexican kid of the group and he shook his big head, no.

Ra-tat-tat-tat-tat-tat! Bloc! Bloc! Bloc! Bloc! Six Mexicans hopped out as four of them was shooting pistols and assault rifles. The two armless Mexicans ran and snatched Taqiq A male teacher tried to save him until his body was riddled with bullets.

The screams, yells, and chaos could be heard miles away as kids and adults tried to take cover. The van burnt rubber flying down the street, speeding over speed bumps and passing stop signs and red lights.

The teachers called the police. They could hear sirens nearing the scene. There were eight dead bodies—three teachers who tried to protect the children and five kids who were all dead on the hot pavement stretched out.

***

Less than six minutes later, Lil Ali pulled up to the block the school was on to see police, ambulance workers, and firefighters surrounding the block.

Lil Ali wasted no time as he hopped out and walked under the yellow tape to see people crying and screaming.

"Excuse me, sir, what happened? My little brother goes to this school," he said to one of the cops standing around, shaking his head at all the white sheets wrapped up in bodies in all sizes.

"Eight dead kids and teachers—it was a terrifying scene, kid," the cop said as the school principal approached them.

"Ali, I'm so sorry. Let him in please. They took Taqiq," he said as Lil Ali stood there with tears forming in his eyes, not knowing what to say because he was so shocked.

"Sir, are you okay? We need to ask you some questions if you don't mind," the cop said as he told the news reporters taking pictures and trying to get under the yellow tape, to capture some of the long story.

The principal guided Lil Ali to the detectives standing around, trying to figure this out as the forensic team did their job talking bias, shell cases for DNA, and every dead victim's blood sample.

Lil Ali answered the simple questions the cops were asking like Taqiq's age, birth, height, address and of course does he have any enemies they should know of! When he asked whether they had any gunmen, they told him all the Mexicans got away with his brother from the footage.

After thirty minutes of nothing, he took a couple of cards as they promised to put out a missing person report. He was walking back to his car to see his mom calling as he answered.

"Taqiq—where is he? Is he with you? I just saw the news!" Ayesha yelled as Lil Ali was silent.

"Mom, some Mexicans kidnapped him," he replied as Ayesha yelled and cried through the phone for her baby. Lil Ali pulled off with tears, ready to kill whoever had something to do with his brother's kidnapping.

***

South Philly

"Uhmmm—" slurping noises could be heard all through the small one-bedroom apartment as Melody bopped her head up and down on Jamel's dick.

She deep-throat every inch without gagging, vomiting or choking; she relaxed her throat and worked her wet warm mouth.

"Damn!" Jamel moaned, leaning his head back, feeling the coke he just hit. She spit on his dick as she massaged his saggy balls, as her blonde hair flew everywhere all over the bed.

His pre-cum started to fill her mouth as she worked his pole, as she sucked his tip while doing tongue tricks. He busted a load of thick cum down her throat as she swallowed all his kids.

Melody stood up, showing her naked petite body. Her breasts were saggy—DD breasts with pierced nipples. She was forty-one years old, small, with blue glossy eyes, a pretty youthful face and a soft body. Her pussy and head game was top-notch. She only fucked with black males; she was a pale white woman and liked her men dark chocolate.

Jamel got dressed and took a hit of pure Colombian coke that was on his dresser sitting on a glass mirror. His mother passed a couple of weeks ago and since then he been drugging harder and harder as if life had no meaning to it anymore. To make matters worse, he felt as if he let Ali down because Taqiq was kidnapped and Lil Ali was all over the news.

He knew it was someone powerful to get past Ayesha's skillful training, which made him more worried about their safety. He knew he had to get the monkey off his back and find the kid and Ayesha, to keep his promise to Ali.

Lately he'd been extremely paranoid but he thought it was because of the coke and crack he was using daily to hide the pain. Jamel hit another line and his dick grew harder as he saw Melody lube her asshole as she bent over on all fours.

"Come fuck me," she said as Jamel already had his dick in his hand, stroking it as he made his way to her. He rammed his dick into her ass, and she screamed while gripping his dirty shirts, feeling him rip her and open. He started fucking the life outta of her as the room started to smell like musk, as they both climaxed before Melody had to go teach her third grade class.

Chapter Sixteen

Ayesha and Jamel had been hanging out a lot daily, enjoying each other's company. Prior to the time Taqiq was kidnapped, she'd agreed to visit Jamel in his crib. Although she had yet to recover from the shock of her son's kidnap, she went ahead to visit Jamel, at least by way of releasing some pent-up anger and frustration. This was their seventh date. Jamel begged her to come to his house, and now they were together cuddled up as she was under his big arm.

Jamel rubbed her soft legs to feel smooth skin then he kissed her neck softly, smelling her Prada perfume as she tilted her head back and let out a soft moan. He was so horny for her. He'd been picturing her in his dreams lately and he knew tonight was the night.

Ayesha uncrossed her legs as his hand went up her thighs, as her pussy was dripping wet as he teased her. Jamel stopped and pulled out her nice perky breasts and started to suck on her firm breasts.

"Uhmmm, yeah!" she moaned as her dress was soaked with her wetness because she wore no panties. He licked her soft nipples quickly in anticipation. As he licked and sucked, she lifted her dress over her head, leaving on only her heels.

When Jamel saw her six-pack and curves, he was shocked but the sight of her pussy had his dick about to bust. Her pussy was so phat and small as if a finger would have trouble entering. She had clear cum dripping down her upper thighs.

He got on his knees between her legs and attacked her pussy with his mouth as she moaned in appreciation while he teased her small swollen clit by flicking his tongue on it. Her hips started to move with his tongue tracing her slit as he fingered her love box.

"Ohhh shit—yesss—I'm cu-m-in!" she moaned before cuming back to back in his mouth as she drenched his face with her sweet cum.

"Ummm, you taste good," he said as she was taking deep breaths because she was in ecstasy.

"My turn," he said while he stood up unbuckling his slacks, pulling out the biggest dick she ever saw. Ayesha's eyes were wide open. His dick was so long that she knew he would rip her kidneys open if he put that monster in her.

Jamel sat down and guided her hand to his dick, stroking it.

"Hold on," she said and stood ass naked as she walked to the table for a sip of water. He watched her ass wiggle and her perfect tits bounce with each step. He couldn't wait to feel her tight pussy. His finger was hurting trying to finger her pussy.

Ayesha walked back towards him, looking at his massive hard dick. She climbed on him and lost no time in riding his dick. His moans and hers were in sync as she rode his dick harder, then she leaned forward and bit his neck. At first, he thought it was a mere love bite but when she bit him again—this time savagely and ferociously—he yelled in agony, seeing her mouth stained with his blood. "What the hell was that for?" he said as she got off of him. "Are you a vampire or something?"

"Maybe," Ayesha spat, getting dressed. "Look, I think we should stop seeing each other anymore and don't bother calling me again," she added and left as if nothing happened.

Hours Later

Ayesha sat on her red prayer rug in the middle of her living room floor staring out the glass slide door that led to the small backyard.

The police just left minutes ago to inform her about her son's kidnapping and how they were doing everything to get him back. The gruesome murders at the school made national news, as well as the kidnapping but no names were giving on the public news.

"I can't believe this—outta forty kids to snatch why Taqiq, mom?" Lil Ali said as he walked in the living room scrolling through his social media to see the shooting was the talk of the day as family and friends posted pictures of the loved ones that fell vicitim.

"I'ma ask you a question, be honest, were you involved with any Mexicans or any people that have any dealings with them?"

Ayesha asked in a low pitch voice while looking at a photo of Taqiq when he was younger she kept on the living room oakwood table.

"No, mom, I carefully did my homework before I did anything and I'll never lead anything back to you or Taqiq," he said, looking into her glassy gray eyes.

"I'm just asking but it's not me I'm worrying about. Taqiq is an innocent baby," she replied as she heard a noise she hasn't heard in years. Her old work phone was ringing—a prepaid tracfone she used when she was a hit woman. She got the phone out her purse on the dining room table as Lil Ali wondered where the unfamiliar sound was coming from.

"Who's this?" Ayesha asked.

"Still feisty, long time no speak, Ayesha. How do you like North Carolina? Smart hideout, I must say, but I told you I'll find you if it's the last thing I will do. I kept my promise. I guess you ain't keep yours. Anyway, how did you like my movie earlier? He looks just like you!" the deep voice said that gave her chills.

"Don't you fucking touch him or I fucking swear—"

"Wow! Slow down. I don't want him. He not a threat. A fair exchange will do you for him," the voice said, and it was as though she could see his grin through the phone.

"Deal. Don't touch my son!" she demanded.

"Kids aren't my M.O. but I'm sure you can find me. I'm in the States, Ayesha" the voice said as he hung up in her ear as she tried to hold her tears back.

"What's wrong? Who was that?" Lil Ali said as he listened in on the whole call, as he saw something he never saw in his mother: murder, rage, and pain.

"The wetbag who got my son and who killed your father," she said sadly because she should have killed him but she gave up because she had them to raise.

"What—I thought you told me the man who killed daddy was murdered," he said, pissed off.

"I had to tell you that to protect you. Ole Bay is a very danger-ous man. I'm sorry but it was my job to kill him for Ali honor but I

115

couldn't spend the rest of my life hunting him down and I had two kids to raise," Ayesha said in her defense.

"So raw he's back for our bloodline. I just feel as if there is so much stuff I don't know about my father and his death. I feel like I'm left in the blind and now this nigga got my brother," Lil Ali said, sitting down on a stool in the kitchen.

"You're grown now and you know the streets so I'ma tell ya the whole story. Just be ready to know you never had a regular family," Ayesha said as she began telling him the story of his father from his Philly days to his death. She also told him about Ole Bay— head of a major cartel family.

***

Mexico

Ole Bay laid in his king-size bed on his 2.9-million-dollar yacht that was eighty-five feet with 15 knots under electric power while using a caterpillar engine. The yacht was large and beautiful. The solar area had white thick furry carpet with white leather couches, spin chairs, a glass bar fully loaded with expensive wine and liquor. The wheelhouse and the large lounge was on the upper deck with shiny wooden floors, a sundeck to tan and a master cabin that held sixteen guests.

Ole Bay laid back comfortably with his legs cocked open naked as two beautiful women from the Virgin Islands, St. Lucia took turns sucking his dick to end their four-day orgy.

After he busted a load, both women shared his cum as if it was holy water. The women stood up to leave, ass-naked, going to get a suntan on their pale skin.

Ole Bay got dressed in his Versace silk button-up and slack, looking at the gray wallpaper as he was walking towards the room window. He looked through the crystal clear water on his way in New Mexico–his new home since he emerged from Mexico two years ago to take control of his drug trade in the southwest.

He had been watching Ayesha for twenty minutes waiting on his time to attack and he knew the easiest way to get to a Queen is to get to her prince. He knew the kidnapping would be simple and would get her attention and she would easily deliver herself to him Knowing how deadly she was, he made it his job to cover all tracks and keep his army on standby. He held Taqiq in his safe house surrounded by men; he kept at least fourteen with him at all times. They were all on the lower deck.

Ayesha played in his dreams every night, interrupting his sleep, because he feared she was coming for him. But now he planned to put her out of her misery just like he did Ali—her husband.

***

Lil Ali sat there frozed like an ice cube after hearing the backstory of his father, grandfather, his mother being a FBI agent turned crockett, Ayesha being a trained assassin, all the murders and wars she and his father was in side by side.

"Damn! So what's our plan now?" he asked as she took a sip of tea, looked out the glass window to see a half moon and stars bunched up in the dark sky.

"I'm going to do whatever to get my baby back," she said, sitting straight up.

"I'm coming," he replied.

"No the hell you not. This isn't your fight. I'ma need you to look after Taqiq. God forbid something happens," she said, looking at him seriously, letting him know this was a different type of league.

"He is my brother by blood and religion. I have a right to fight in the cause of him and I'm not taking no for an answer," he demanded.

"I just don't think it's a good idea. I know you're well trained but I can't have your blood on my hands," she responded, shaking her head.

"Let me be the judge of that. Allah will protect us and I think the feds want me for questions after what happened with Bundles," he said, not wanting to go too deep into it to worry her because there was a lot going on already.

"I told you about him. You can't trust these disbelievers," she said, pissed off because she could read between the lines. She could tell Bundles wasn't built for jail; he was just in the streets to chase a name and clout until shit got real. Ayesha understood the streets.

"It's going to be good, mom," he said, rubbing her shoulders.

"Pack up, we're leaving tomorrow so handle all of your needs and wants because there is a good chance we won't be back," she said, getting up from the round glass table, walking to her room. Lil Ali went to his room, fell on his bed thinking about his little brother and revenge on his behalf.

Chapter Seventeen

Cumberland Jail

Bundles lay on his thin mattress on the cold steel bunk as the cold air gave him the chills as he read a hood novel called "A Gangsta Qu'ran".

Tears rolled down his face as he thought about Lil Ali and what he did to him by putting the feds and DEA on him. It's been over a couple of weeks but the guilt was still fresh on his mind because turning on someone so loyal was the worst betrayal of them all.

After his hours of testimonies, the government and the feds promised him sixteen years in federal prison which meant he would have to go to a drop-out yard, also known as a rat yard, for inmates. The worst part would be taking the stand or Lil Ali looking him in his eyes while ending the life of the only person he called a brother.

The feds were building a firm case against Lil Ali with all the information Bundles assisted with. He fell asleep thinking about his little sister, trying to convince himself he was doing the right thing.

***

Nicole woke up out of her sleep to hear someone tossing rocks at her window at twelve at night. She was lucky her mom was a heavy deep sleeper.

Nicole saw Lil Ali standing in her backyard dressed in all black like a ninja. She was confused as to why he ain't call first as he always did on their late night booty calls.

She told him to climb the white ladder attached to her window. She was worried about him. She saw the school shooting on the news and Taqiq being kidnapped. This is her first time seeing Lil Ali since that day she spoke to him a couple of times but she knew he needed space.

Looking into her mirror, she started to fix her curly hair while putting down her see-through nightgown that had her breasts exposed.

"Hey, baby," she stated as he entered her room to see her pink night light on and an apple cinnamon candle burning, giving the room a strong apple scent.

"What's good, boo?" he said, kissing her lips, hugging her tightly.

"I'm sorry to hear about Taqiq, baby, I know they're going to find him," she said as they both laid in her unmade bed.

"It's all in Allah's hands but I'm here to tell yo' me and my mom are leaving town for a while," he said, looking at her worried eyes.

"Okay, how long?" she replied, thinking it was a good idea for them to get away on a vacation.

"I don't know—it could be permanent. It's a lot of shit going but I promise to find my way back to you," he said as she began to cry as her thoughts went wild.

"What if you don't then what?" she said softly, looking at a photo of them both on her nightstand.

"I love you, Nicole, I swear to Allah I'll be back," he said, wiping her tears away.

"Okay," she said as they kissed deeply, as he slipped her nightgown over her head to see her firm large breasts sitting in his face while he undressed.

She opened her thick yellow legs as she laid on her back, showing her phat pretty shaved pussy as her large clit was swollen. He climbed between her legs as he entered his hard dick in her soft, warm tight-grip pussy, slowly stroking as her wetness coated his dick as he went deeper.

"Uhmmm, yesss, daddy, I love you!" she moaned as his balls slapped against the bottom of her wide ass faster and faster until she came like a river.

He placed her right leg over his shoulder and rammed his dick as deep as he could with a rhythm. She started to go crazy feeling his entire length in her kidneys and ribs as he beat her pussy up the way she likes it. The friction of his jack hammer momentum caused her tight pussy to spasm and contract around his massive hard dick.

Her head was spinning as he thrust deep in her soaked pussy as she came twice, making her slit more slippery.

He wrapped his muscular arms around her then rolled her over and pulled her on top so she could ride. She saddled on his dick as he rubbed her big tits that bounced with every move, as she bounced on his dick slowly as it disappeared in her.

"Ug-h-h-h, fu-c-kk me!" she moaned as she leaned forward and started twerking on his dick like it was a pole as he gripped her waist, guiding her up and down. After rotating her thick hips side to side in a powerful motion while riding like a cowgirl, they cum hard and outta breath.

"Goddamn!" she said as they cuddled next to each other's sweaty bodies.

"You know I'm coming back for this fire ass pussy," he said, putting his finger in her warm still wet pussy.

"Nigga, please you better come back—period, and a bitch know I'ma be sore tomorrow," she said, chuckling, letting him play with her pussy as she stared to get horny again.

"Your phone ringing" Nicole said, pissed because she was just about to suck his dick and balls for round two, but his phone going off on the floor fucked her mood up.

"Damn!" He climbed out of bed naked and picked up his phone to see it was Taqiq babysitter who was also their next door neighbor.

"Hello," he answered, listening to her talk so fast he told her to slow down. "Damn, are you sure?" he asked as the babysitter told him fifty agents just raided his house. She asked him what was going on but before he could respond he hung up.

"Fuck!" he said, thinking how he was going to get to the hotel where Ayesha was awaiting him without getting snatched by the pigs.

"So this is why you leaving? Why did the Feds raid your home?" she asked as she overheard the loud woman's every word on the phone.

"Listen, if the police or anybody questions you, tell them nothing except we went to school and we were friends if that," he said, getting dressed as she sat up.

"I'm no dummy. I'll protect you with my life but tell me what's going on and I want to go with you," she said, putting on her gown.

"Noo, yo' can't, baby, some serious shit is going on. I'll be back, trust me," he said, handing her his red, brown, and black Muslim *dhikr* beads.

"Okay. I love you," she said, knowing whatever was going on was dangerous and had to do with Taqiq.

"I love you more," he said as he kissed her and left the same way he sneaked in, as she watched him.

***

Lil Ali made it back to the hotel safely in his new Dodge Viper to see Ayesha's Porsche 911 Turbo all red fresh off the lot parked in front of their room. The hotel parking was packed with travelers, so they thought the cheap but decent hotel was perfect. They traded their cars for something new, faster, and more suitable for traveling in style on their trip.

He left his draco under his seat as he had two pistols glued to his hips. He sat in his car for a second just rethinking everything going on in his young life. Bundles crossed him, the feds were on him, his brother was kidnapped by the cartel, the person who murdered his father now wanted his mother, and Nicole was alone. It was a lot to bear but he knew Allah would give him the strength to get through it; of course it was all a test.

Chapter Eighteen

Ayesha sat in the hotel room reading her noble Qu'ran, gathering her thoughts as Lil Ali took a shower. It was two in the morning and neither one of them could sleep, too much on both of their minds.

The hotel room was small mainly for travelers or one night stands. The room had two queen-size beds, two old marble wood dressers with an oversize, overheated lamp, a small 17-inch TV, yellow wallpaper that needed a new layer due to wear and tear and, of course, a small one-person fit bathroom.

She knew her family's life was in danger. She thought of every way she could kill Ole Bay once and for all and get her son back alive. It was going to be hard but she knew she had to do something.

Just as her mind started to wander, the sight of the morning now distracted her attention when she saw a familiar block. Within seconds she saw federal agents walking in and out of her house as the news reported, stating there was a manhunt for a man who is responsible for more than three murders and he lived in the house behind her.

Ayesha's heart froze as a high school picture of Lil Ali popped up on the screen saying, *armed and dangerous.*

This was too much for her to bear; she couldn't let the police take her son. Her mind went crazy as she turned off the TV. She chose this hotel on the outskirts of Fayetteville to avoid any attention, and she was glad she did because she knew the police had the city on lock.

"Damn!" she said as the shower in the bathroom turned off. She wondered if he knew he was wanted for murders. She was glad he came back on time from visiting Nicole or it may have been too late. She made a quick *Dua* asking Allah to forgive her for her sins and protect her child from all evil.

Ten minutes later, Lil Ali walked in the room in a black tank top and basketball shorts dancing to his iPad. He saw Ayesha's long silky hair and her smooth skin in her night pajamas looking amazing with no make-up, but he could tell by the look on her face she was displeased with something.

"Do you have anything to tell me?" she asked, staring at the old-fashioned drapes.

"Yes, I'm sorry I made a mistake and now the feds are looking for me," he said as he took a seat on the edge of her bed.

"I always taught you to do shit by yourself. Now look, it could cost you your life. Non-believers are not your friends," she said, taking a deep breath, frustrated as he just listened knowing he slipped up big time.

"It's okay," she said as she took it easy on him. "We all make mistakes and as a family, one fall—we all fall and rise in the name of Allah. Now go to sleep. We got a long trip," she said, climbing under her covers. Lil Ali went to go make his late night prayer, remembering Ramadan starts in less than twenty-four hours.

***

Fayetteville State College

Nicole was in her art & design class listening to students talk about the ATT homecoming games in Greensboro—the biggest game in the state. The teachers received a call and told her to report to the dean's office for whatever reasons.

She left class walking through the shiny hallways full of lockers and students' art work. The art building was located by the administration office. Her trip to the dean's office was short as she traveled in the Chanel sundress and flip flops, feeling the summer heatwave scorch the pavement.

Walking into the administration brick building, she felt the A/C chill her body off within seconds as she tried to figure out what this was about. Lately she been heavy on prescription drugs to block her depression and her suicidal thoughts. Since seeing her lover on the news wanted for murders last week, her emotions been in shiggles and her friends could read her like an open book.

She saw the wooden door that led to the dean's office open. Three people were inside the room; the dean of the college and two people dressed in suits she never saw—a male and female.

"Nicole, good afternoon," Ms. Galigion—the counselor—said, seated at the polished red oakwood table next to Mr. Belment—the school Dean—and a white man and Spanish woman both staring at her, trying to reach her.

"Hey, what is this about if I may ask? I have exams my next class," she said as she took a seat at the far end wondering the what the fuck was going on.

"We're sorry for interrupting you, just to clarify that, but this here is my partner—Agent McKinnon—and my name is Agent Camilla, and were investigating a yang man by the name of Ali Jr Braxten who is wanted for murders," Ms. Camilla stated, tapping her manicured nails on the table.

Nicole was ready to get up and walk out. "Now Nicole these good folks are only here to ask you a couple of questions," McGaligion said in her country voice.

"Look, we know you have dealing with him and he is a very dangerous young man," Agent McKinnon said, looking at her facial expression change.

"Since when was it illegal to text? I've known him since the third grade, everybody does, and he is a good person so y'all can miss me with all that bullshit!" she stated firmly as the ghetto fabulous came outta her as she rolled her neck and eyes.

"It's not legal but when you have dealings with a murderer on the run. You're now an association but we don't want to pressure you, so whenever you feel like you're ready to talk, give us a call," Agent Camilla said as she pushed her card down the table.

"Okay," Nicole said, standing up to leave, not even picking up the card.

"She's a good girl, she will come around. She is one of our smartest students. I can assure you she will," the dean said, leaning back in the recliner chair in his gray suit texting her brother-in-law for a golf trip.

***

Once the agents made it outside, the heat turned up on them as they were walking through the mob of students on the manicured grass.

"I know she is lying. She is trying to protect him; such a pretty girl falling for the wrong type. I was there once before," Agent Camilla said, thinking about her high school and college days in New York, the Bronx, where she was originally from.

"We just gotta watch her closely. I know she knows a lot more," Agent McKinnon said.

"Yeah, of course, but did they ever look into his little brother kidnapping? Because I believe this is bigger than what we see," she said as she opened the door to the GMC truck.

Ms. Camilla was beautiful at twenty-nine, no kids, no marriage, Dominican, short, and brown hair, hazel almond eyes, petite frame, toned body, round ass, and she was a Bronx boomer. After graduating college at Duke, she went to the police academy at twenty-one and passed with flying colors. Now she was an agent who loved her job unlike her partner.

McKinnon was forty-six years old with a youthful appearance, who stood out in shape. He was married with two kids. He had twenty-two years as an agent so he was well trained. He kept Camilla on her toes.

"Everything will come to light but no signs of the Taqiq kid or the Mexicans who did the shit. The captain is still on our ass," he said, driving off the school campus to get lunch.

Chapter Nineteen

Abu Dhabi

Cattolina sat in the back of her polished white Maybach Ghost, one of her many luxury foreign cars she had. She was looking through her tints at the beautiful city that she'd loved since she was a kid when her—aunt Hadrat—raised her out here as well as the big city of Oman.

Her chauffeur and bodyguard, Mr. Uttiman, a large Muslim man trained to kill, guided the Maybach through the city streets, passing white sand beaches and camel riders on the side of the road. She thought of her aunty who was murdered by her sister—Ayesha—over ten years ago. She missed Hadrat, who taught her everything she needed to know in life—from her deadly murder skills, business, seduction, honor and success.

Also Hurayra, her father, didn't want her so he gave her to his younger sister, Hadrat, to raise because another daughter wasn't in his plans. When her birth mother was murdered at the age of two, Cattolina was under Hadrat's authority who was wealthy at a young age from inheritances.

They drove past her favorite building—the Burj Khalifa—which was the world's tallest building standing at 2722 foot touching the clear blue skies. A half block down was her favorite place to shop and as well as everyone else in Dhabi. The Dubai Mall was the second biggest mall in the world; some people would come from all over the world just to walk around.

Cattolina was twenty-six years old and one of the wealthiest women in the United Arab Emirates, thanks to what her aunty left her. She owned resorts, clubs, yachts, mansions, two private jets, and a casino that was doing very well since it opened last year but it couldn't compare to the Sahih casino that she and Ali owned but she had no clue who ran it.

The scorching desert weather and dust storms made Dhabi the golden falcon city—its nickname. She hated she had to leave but she had to go find the person who haunted her dreams for years—Ayesha.

She carried a picture of her sister around daily; she looked like her a little but one couldn't tell they were real sisters.

Cattolina was an Arabian goddess with golden bronze skin, gray and green eyes, thick full lips, smooth curves, five-five height, weighing a hundred and twenty pounds, flat stomach and nice small pointy breasts. She was born a Muslim like everyone else in the Middle East but she didn't practice or care for religion. She lived by her own rules. She killed when she wanted and fucked when she wanted.

The Maybach arrived on the private runway where her private jet was waiting on her with two SUVs full of goons climbing out with assault rifles to patrol the area for their sexy boss.

This trip was important; she was going to America to find Ayesha to kill her once and for all because she couldn't live on this earth knowing she was still out there. There was also more reason as she wanted her sister dead but when the time came, she would tell her face to face as she delivered her death. She was well aware of Ayesha's skills but she knew she was better especially hearing about how she let some cartel family murder her husband in cold blood, she considered Ayesha weak.

The kidnapping of her son seen all across the world is what brought her attention to North Carolina where Ayesha was hiding all these past years.

Thank you, Uttiman, I got it from here. I will see you upon my return," she said in her strong Middle Eastern voice as he just nodded.

She stepped out with her six-inch red bottom heels clicking on the hot pavement, wearing a white mini dress by Saint Laurent showing her perfect curves and figure. She walked inside her jet like a diva as her guards made their way back in their SUV as the jet's staircase closed in with the jet entrance.

***

Nicole was sitting on the cushion bathroom toilet biting her fingernails, staring at the pregnancy test on the mobile sink.

She missed her period, which never happened and lately she had been feeling dizzy, tired, and weak so her roommate told her she should pick up a pregnancy test.

She checked her watch and the ten minutes was up as she picked the test up and screamed when she saw it read positive. She smiled but when she thought about Lil Ali's situation, she frowned because what if she had to raise a child on her own. One thing for certain: she refused to get rid of the unborn seed growing in her that belonged to the man she truly loved.

Nicole flushed the test, washed her hands and exited the bathroom to see her mom standing on the other side of the door with a pregnancy test box in her hand with an evil look on her white pale face.

"What do you want me to say? I'm pregnant by Ali, mom," Nicole said as she walked towards her room.

"Are you totally stupid? The man is wanted for murders. He's all over the news. Wait until I tell your father, young lady!" she shouted as Nicole slammed her door shut.

***

Albuquerque, New Mexico

Lil Taqiq sat on his small twin size bunk bed watching cartoon in the same Muslim garment he wore for weeks now. The room was in the basement of one of Ole Bay's mansions he rarely used. The room had no window, no bathroom, only a bunk bed, toilet near the metal entrance door, a small TV on top of milk carts, toys, kid books, and a small lamp. The guards fed him three meals through the door slot like a real prisoner and for his rec they would slide him a Xbox and games he can play for two hours a day.

Taqiq was quiet during his stay. He was traumatized after seeing all his classmates gunned down in broad daylight. He knew he was being held against his own will because he overheard the kidnappers talking to each other as they were bringing him downstairs.

Everyday he prayed the men with the guns would let him go free back home to his mom and his brother.

***

Brooklyn, NY

Face leaned back in his all-red Maserati Ghibli with black rims and black leather interior seats. Two cars tailed him as he rode through the streets of his hometown—Brooklyn, East New York. Face was at Kingpin status at thirty years old, following in his father Havoc footsteps who was a member of the Black Mafia crew out in Philly.

Face ran dope and coke from NY to Texas with his crew of Bloods; he ran because he had his own set. He had law enforcement, mainly NYPD, under his belt on the payroll to keep him ahead of the game. Within the next twenty-four hours Face had to make a trip to Philly to meet with his connect—Abdul Rahmin—who was good friends with his father before he was murdered.

Before his trip to Philly he had to go see Bones—his capo—and Flatbush and Fulton who handled all his dirty work.

***

Flatbush Ave was packed with niggas hanging out with blue flags representing their crip set. This was Bones Black; he was the big Crip at 5 ft. He was the big homie around this way. Bones was Face capo even though he was crippin and Face was blooded, the two were childhood friends. The two were like Supreme and Prince back in the day but more deadly and richer.

"You what's good, son?" Face said as he hopped out wearing a Balmain outfit and shoe to match with two Cuban link rope chains on, as his goons waited outside the Benz and BMW.

"Mobbing out here, fam, ready to hit same clubs up later on in Queens with the locs from the 90'z," Bones said, leaning on his QX50 Infiniti navy blue truck with blue and cream two tone interior, looking fresh in his white paris jeans and top.

"I mean to scream at you, son, what's happened with Thug and PG in the Bronx? I gave you full control of the Bronx, my nigga, them niggas having short cuts and we all on the same team," Face said, referring to the shot cuts he been hearing about with there workers for the Bronx, Highbridge section.

"I'll take care of it, cuz, no issue you heard," Bones said in his smooth voice. "I'ma bail out Manny from the Island on Monday. They gave him bail on the murder rape he took for Loice," Bones said, referring to Face little cousin who was Bones' drop.

"Cool because I'ma go check and go holla at my people in Philly," Face said, giving Bones a look letting him know to hold it down till he got back.

"Bout time, cuz, I'm almost dry. These niggas moving pie like girl scout cookies, my nigga," Bones said, letting a blunt of good weed as the hood was so noisy he could barely hear himself talk.

"I be knowing just no killing until I get back—we got enough going on," Face said, walking off, knowing Bones was a cold-blooded murderer—one of the most ruthless niggas in BK, with a shortman complex.

Romell Tukes

Chapter Twenty

N.C. F.B.I.

"Captain, I've done some more research on this Ali kid, come to find out he was the best martial art fighter in the state. I've spoken to some of his students, but—sad to say—they all speak highly of him. Then to make shit more sad—he was an honor student with a bright college future. Just give us a little more time but the only thing we have on him is *he say she say*," Agent Camilla said, seated in the Captain's office, the Captain listening to one of his best agents.

"This shit is costing me a lot of time. We have a murderer on the run. I don't give a fuck if he was Bruce Lee brother or with an IQ of 4.4. I gave you this case. People above me are asking questions and I don't like to be questioned!" Captain Ford stated sarcastically, taking off his glasses.

Capital Ford was sixty-four years old and close to retirement. He was a grumpy old white man, married with three children—all of them work in law enforcement.

"Yes, sir, I will work harder," she said, standing up, fixing her navy blue skirt and DKNY blouse with six-inch heels showing her sexy smooth legs.

Camilla went back to her booth trying to think around the nosey agents screaming and yelling every second as if they were still in high school.

"Guess what?" Agent McKinnon said as he approached her in a suit and tie with a folder in his hand.

"I'm not in the mood for the guessing game," she said.

"Ohhh, someone missed their period—gosh! Lighten up a little. Anyway, I traced the back history of this kid and come to find out he was the son of the famous Ali—the one who went from druglord to big casino owner until he was murdered. He was on the red radar for years all over the States from Philly to Miami, but they were never able to snatch him. He was the real deal!" Mckinnon said, dropping the folder on her desk.

"I heard of the case, I believe. So you think the kidnapping of the little kid has something to do with it also?" she asked, looking at the blueprint.

"Maybe—maybe," he said as Camilla sat there thinking so hard she felt a headache, knowing she was missing pieces to the puzzle.

***

Philly

Face walked in the nice quiet park and sat on the green bench, looking into bright morning skies to feel that morning breeze, at six in the morning.

This was one of the spots he would meet his connect, always; he would conduct business in the mornings in a quiet public area. Face left his soldiers at the hotel except his two most loyal men who were parked at the end of the block watching his back.

Moments after, all-black tinted SUV trucks pulled up as if the president was arriving any second in North Philly.

Abdul Rahimin hopped out one of the parked trucks alone wearing an Armani suit and tie with a long salt-and-pepper beard with a black kufi. Abdul was fifty-three years old and the new King-pin of the whole Philly from North to West. He had an army of Muslims all over the city ready to kill at his will. When he came home seven years ago from his sixteen-year federal bid, he met a connect and his life changed forever.

"Peace, yang brother," Abdul said as he embraced Face, as the goose chased each other around the wet grass.

"I'm okay, how are you?" Face replied as both men took a slow walk down the pier by the small lake.

"Blessed. Allah is with me but I'm glad you're here. There is something I want to bring to your attention that has nothing to do with our business," Abdul said.

"Okay," Face stated.

"You remember the name Ali?" Abdul asked in his low pitch voice.

"Of course, who doesn't? I met him years ago when I first got in the game through my old connect—Fatal," he said.

"Good. Well, he was murdered while I was in prison. I was friends with his father, but he left two kids behind and one was recently kidnapped and one is wanted for murders," he stated sadly.

"Damn, that's fucked up. I know if he was alive he'd turn the city up, but all due respect—why does this concern me?" Face asked.

"It has a lot to do with you, my friend, because the man who caused all this mayhem is out for bloodlines and I believe you're next on his list, brother, but that's not the worst," he said as Face had a confused look on his face, not understanding.

"The man is the one who murdered your father," Abdul said, now getting his full attention as his body tensed up.

"Ole Bay—" Face stated with an evil look full of hate, envy, and hurt. He wanted to catch Ole Bay for years but he knew going up against one of the biggest cartel leaders in the world was a lose-lose situation.

"Why is he just popping up now after ten years?" Face asked.

"I don't know but if I was you I wouldn't wait around to find out," Abdul said, taking a deep breath.

"I understand. I'll figure this shit out. Where is he at now?" he asked.

"Word is he lives in New Mexico now with a bigger real-estate than he got in Mexico full of soldiers. I deal with associates of his on business. This is how I know this information but these are deadly dangerous people. They took out Ali and your father, so just be smart. If there is anything I can do, call me. I'll do what I can. I am a businessman but I'm also a family man first, and Havoc and Ali were like family to me," Abdul said sternly.

Chapter Twenty-One

North Carolina

Cattolina was sitting on the motel bed on her laptop, scrolling through Nicole's Facebook and IG account, looking at her photos. It was nine in the morning. Her flight landed seventy hours ago. She chose a motel in Fort Bragg; of course she used a fake military ID to get into the gated city.

So she saw pictures of Nicole and Lil Ali together and they were cute together. She had to admit her nephew was a very handsome young man. Cattolina was looking for one thing, and that was any type of location of Nicole's last posts. All she saw was pics from her school campus.

Minutes later she saw a photo of her standing in a driveway in front of a Lexus in a white bodycon suit with clear Versace heels. Cattolina zoomed in on the background of the house.

"Bingo! Mission complete," she said as she wrote down the house number. She closed her laptop and got undressed and walked to the shower naked as her breasts and ass jiggled with every step.

The hot water was a perfect temperature as she climbed inside the shower and closed the glass door as steam filled the bathroom, fogging the windows and mirror. Cattolina's body was toned, soft, and smooth as she rubbed Dove body wash towards her thin Brazilian wax hair then back up to her small lite brown nipples as the soap soothed her body. Cattolina placed her finger in her pussy, rubbing her clit, playing in her tight pussy as her wetness built up as she moaned. When she felt herself about to cum, her body tensed up, then she came hard as she squirted on the shower floor as her cum came out like waterholes for twenty seconds.

"Ugghh, fuck!" she moaned as water soaked her long hair, touching the snake tattoo on her lower back.

After twenty-five minutes of washing herself up, she got dressed casually in a pair of tight jeans and a Gucci blouse to match her good heels and sunglasses. It was 96° outside. She already hated the dirty south heat; it was a lot different from desert heat.

She grabbed her Gucci logo purse and placed a baby 9mm inside and a Mini Ruger 14 carbine with 223 remington with a silencer and extended clip to attach to it. She looked at herself in the mirror and smiled at how beautiful she was, as she always did.

***

Thirty Minutes Later

Cattolina was driving towards Tiffany Pines in a royal blue Hyundai sedan she was renting. She used her GPS to guide her through the city. This was her second time in America and she knew she stood out like a sore thumb with her Arabian features.

The city was small but nice. She saw the large Fort Bragg base, the armory, clothing stores, commissary, the military PX and many restaurants up and down the streets.

Cattolina was glad to have a firm location on Nicole because going to her school was out of the question especially with all the school shootings she saw on the news about Americans.

She finally made it to Nicole's block to see the black Kia she saw in a lot of Nicole pics with her friends parked in the driveway. Cattolina parked at the end of the block, grabbed a clipboard and changed into a Marines uniform she bought at the PX yesterday. She didn't think it would be smart to wear the uniform daily because she was Arabian and most would assume she was a Muslim—which wouldn't add up.

***

Nicole sat in her living room watching TV. After the the Oprah Show, she was waiting on the Wendy Williams Show to come on so she could hear all the juicy gossip. Today she chose to stay home because she had a doctor appointment in three hours with her doctor downtown. Lately, her hormones had been taking control of her emotions because not only was she a single mother but school and work had taken a toll on her. Her mother helped her but she was still disappointed in her daughter.

Nicole heard the doorbell ring. She sucked her teeth and fixed her big shirt Ali gave months ago that hid her small pouch.

"Hold on," she said and the person rang it again as she wobbled to the door. When she opened the door, she saw a pretty young woman dressed in her army uniform with a clipboard in hand.

"How may I help you?" Nicole said, praying nothing happened to her father in the army and she was here to deliver the bad news.

"Hi, I'm Lieutenant Godfield and I'm trying to recruit young women such as yourself to join me in the army to fight for our country," Cattolina said in her best American voice.

Nicole took a deep breath glad it wasn't about her father.

"No, Mrs. It's okay. I'm good. I got enough going on," she replied, looking at her gray eyes, trying to see where she knew them from, and her voice was different.

"Alright, thank you, but do you mind if I use your ladies' room? I drove four hours just to recruit people and I don't know where a gas station is around here." Cattolina spoke softly but made sure her tone was laced with emergency.

"Okay, make it fast. My mom will be back soon," Nicole said as she opened the door for her. "It's to your left at the end of the hallway," she said, pointing down the hall, closing the door behind her.

As soon as she turned around, fear took over her.

"Sit down and shut up," Cattolina said, pointing a silencer in her face, watching her sit down slowly.

"Please don't," Nicole said, crying, feeling dizzy.

"Where is your handsome boyfriend and his mother my sister?" she asked in her strong Middle Eastern voice

"I—I—I don't know who you're talking about," she said, fumbling over her words.

"Don't lie, honey, don't be a brave little girl," Cattolina stated.

"I just fucking told you, bitch, I don't know or care what the fuck you talking about. I love my man and will always!" Nicole shouted as she spit in the air, catching Cattolina's whole face.

"You fucking bitch!" Cattolina shot her three times in the face before leaving the house.

***

Alamogordo, NM

Ayesha left her Porsche and drove her son's Viper down the dark highways, passing farms and old run-down barns as well as deep caves.

"You okay?" Ayesha asked as she drove down the country roads thinking about Taqiq.

"Just hoping everything will go correct," he said in a flat tone.

"It will, trust Ole Bay. It ain't your brother he really wants. He wants me so he can finally have peace of mind. That's how a coward thinks."

"I'm scared of that too," he said as they turned off a rocky dark dirt road leading to a yellow house forty feet up the road. The house had three pickup trucks parked in the lot belonging to some extra company. The house was in the cut, hiding behind large trees and a small wood barn hanging on its last wood.

"I'ma take the front acting as if I'm a bill collector and you take the back. There are more people than I imagined, so be careful. Shoot first and ask no questions," she said, wrapping her hair up in a ponytail as Lil Ali admired her gangsta side.

"I got you," he said, hopping out in all black, racing towards the back yards as she hopped out and fixed her blazer before walking on the rocks in her heels with two pistols by her side in their holsters.

Chapter Twenty-Two

Philly

Jamel rushed into his apartment building as if he was running from the police in a dirty champion hoodie and sweatpants. This was his third time coming from the crackhouse down the block where he copped his crack from.

Everything was going bad. He was dead broke. The money left him ran out five months ago. The money from his mother's will was just about done with. He only had forty-five dollars left. His rent was light and he had no help. Melody helped him from time to time until two days ago when he hit her. Crack was taking over him. His jaw twerked all day for a hit.

Once on his floor, he fumbled for his keys. Once in his apartment, a strong odor took over his sense of smell, giving him a headache.

He pulled out two small rocks in a plastic sandwich bag as he turned on the living room lights, remembering where he put his glass pipe at.

"Jamel," a voice said, making him jump out his skin as he reached for his gun he sold for crack a few days ago.

"Ain't no fucking way," Jamel shouted as his heart raced, as he looked at the dude sitting on his couch in a black tailor made suit.

"You let me and my family down. You gave me your word you will protect my family. I gave you two million dollars to look after yourself and stay above water, not fall victim to a crackhead," the man said softly, looking at the crack offered in his hand.

"Ali—I'm s-o-o-rry. I thought you were dead. I did the best I could but how are you here alive?" Jamel said, still shocked Ali was alive and back.

"Long story—a fisherman saved me—a Colombian man got me before the shark did after Ole Bay shot me. You see, I knew what Ole Bay plan was because I been figured out my brother was his son. They had too much in common and he was playing me too close. Well, anyway, the fisherman brought me to Colombia, took me to the hospital and guess who showed up days later! Rigo who ran the Colombian biggest cartel and now I'm here looking for my family." Ali stood up with a pistol in his hand.

"So this is it? Our friendship isn't valuable? Jamel asked, watching the pistol rise slowly.

All that shit died when you turned your back on your family," Ali said before pulling the trigger twice, sending two clean head-shots to the big man's dome.

***

Ali took off, ran down the building and hopped in an all- black E-class benz with white cream interior and woodgrain all over the dashboard.

Ali drove off thinking about ten years ago when Ole Bay shot him off his yacht, leaving him for shark food but Ali was two steps ahead of him. He wore a vest and had a meeting with Rigo days before his meeting. The fisherman was Rigo's worker; he picked Ali up from the middle of the ocean after trailing Ole Bay's boat for hours. Ali knew Rigo was his only choice where he could lay low and fake a death to protect his family from the cartel who wanted him dead.

He was back to get his son and keep his other son outta prison. He didn't want to come back but he had to save his family and kill Ole Bay once and for all. His first stop was New York to speak to a young man by the name of Face who was Havoc's son, and word was he had a big army in New York.

That was the only issue: Ali had no army and he hoped Face would catch him since both men had a similar interest in the same person.

***

New Mexico

"I swear if you fucking move a bone I'll blow both of your brains out," Lil Ali said to the two Mexican men laying on their stomachs on the floor stretched out scared. The men were supposed to be here to protect their boss's wife and kids. Lil Ali heard two shots ring off upstairs. Both men on the floor looked at each other with a crazy face.

Seconds later Ayesha walked in the kitchen behind a beautiful Mexican woman. The lady wore a lingerie set—red and pink—showing her large breasts, small waist, curves and her large camel toe peeking out her panties. The woman cried hard as she sat down next to the men, crying for her twin daughters who was just murdered in their sleep.

"Good, now I got everyone's attention—where is Ole Bay?" Ayesha asked all three of them as they all gave each other an evil look. One of the men told Ole Bay's wife in Spanish he loves her and she shook her head crying. The two have been having an affair for the past year since Ole Bay was never around and not to mention he had another family and wife.

"You got five seconds to start talking, someone?" Ayesha said in Spanish, surprising everyone.

"We don't know nothing, he barely come here," a young handsome Mexican stated, hoping she would spare them—at least him and Eva.

"Okay."

Boom! Boom! Boom! The Ricky Martin look-alike body jerked—as if he was doing a dance—before taking his last breath.

"Now how about you?" she asked the other dude laying there now crying as blood from his cousin squirted on his lips and chin.

"I'm sorry, migo, me know nada," he said before Lil Ali shot him four times in his back as Eva closed her eyes tightly, knowing her life was over

"One little piggy left," Ayesha said, looking at Eva.

"He lives on a yacht. I don't know where his other house is. He keeps it private. Please just leave. You killed my babies and my lover," she said before Ayesha emptied her clip from her P89 Rugar.

"Come," she said, making her way out the front as Lil Ali stepped over blood and bodies, following his mother. He had no clue Ayesha was this ruthless. The sweet lady he was used to seeing everyday turned into a full beast. If he knew her history!

Chapter Twenty-Three

New Mexico

Pedro Armendariz sat in his small personal conference office he used for business purposes and relaxation. The large 5228 square feet mansion was heavily guarded during daytime hours only. At night he felt no need for his men, so they stayed in a mini mansion four doors down the block.

Pedro was the underboss and capo of Ole Bay organization; he mainly controlled the family drug trafficking and business affairs. He was a short Mexican man at five-two, gray hair but clean-cut, fit and he walked with confidence in his designer suits.

He just came back from a big meeting with the Black Hands of California over turf wars and new prices on his shipments he provided to the coast. Lately Pedro had a lot on his plate but one issue that was new to him was the death of his boss's wife and daughters; his heart went out to him.

Yesterday when he talked to Ole Bay, he was positive he knew what this was about: the kid he kidnapped from North Carolina. When Ole Bay told him what he did, Pedro was against it because you should never awake a sleeping dog. Pedro heard of Ali and the deadly woman—Ayesha—who murdered a ton of people in his hometown of Mexico City, Mexico years ago.

With his own family to fend for and look after, Ole Bay issues were drugs, extra baggages, plus now with his marriage on the rocks he had no time for useless activities or worthless issues that would affect business.

His wife, Patricia, was forty-one years old and beautiful; she looked as if she was in her twenties. She won Ms. America growing up. She was Mexican-American raised in Arizona and El Paso, Texas, with her immigrant parents.

"Daddy," a soft voice whispered through the crack of the double doors.

"Yes, sweetie, come in," he said, knowing it was his beautiful daughter, Mary. She walked in looking around the room she rarely saw in her own house because her father kept it locked while he was always out on business trips.

The room had Versace designed rugs, drapes, chairs and a couple of photos of her grandparents she never met. Her father sat behind his round marble oak desk with 24k gold on the outside edges, with his face buried in his computer.

"You busy?" Mary said, now standing in front of him looking beautiful, a younger Patricia.

Mary was five-four in height, light-skinned with a tan, chinky eyes, full thick pink lips, dimples that hugged her bright smile, greenish bright eyes, healthy long silky black hair and a petite frame with a round bubble ass. She was every man's fantasy; she even flirted with her father's guards sometimes. She was only eighteen but carried herself as a woman, seducing any man that came her way.

"No, I'm not. How can I help you, love? You look nice today. Why are you dressed up?" Pedro said as he raised his head towards his daughter who wore a green mini dress made by Saint Laurent that stopped above her knees, and a pair of six-inch pumps showing her manicured toes.

"I'm going out to dinner and movies with Melissa later, papi. I told you but first I want to go get my hair done and pick up mommy's birthday gift before she comes back from her Miami trip tomorrow," she said, still standing up because she was already running late as usual.

"Okay, that's perfect. Just take Mucho and Carlos Jr with you also. You ready for UCLA in two months," Pedro said, smiling proudly; his daughter was on her way to college.

"Yes, papi, but I'ma miss home and my friends," she replied honestly.

"I know you'll be okay. You can always come back home. Now get going. I got business to attend to and put your seatbelt on. I don't need to be paying no more petty tickets," he said, putting his glasses back on, typing into his computer as she walked out.

***

Mary pushed the all-white Benz C63AMG cabriolet caper with a black ragtop that hid in the trunk with a press of a button.

She stopped at a red light, bobbing her head to the new Drake album without her seatbelt on; she was an outlaw. Looking into her rearview mirror, she saw an all-black Jeep Cherokee tailing two cars behind her as the summer heat made her leather seats stick to her skin.

Mary was a party girl with a freaky side but at home she was an angel of course. Her best friends Melissa, Anna, and Jazzy were her day one girls since middle school and they all planned to attend college in two months.

Melissa was white and rich; that was her bestie even though Melissa was a big slut. She let dudes run trains on her, gangbang, threesome; whatever there was to do, she was down. Mary was different; she just loved dark men—African-Americans. If it wasn't chocolate, she ain't want it, and Melissa was the same.

The shopping center was packed with cars coming in and out. She found a parking space and rushed out of her car, already ten minutes late for her hair appointment. She saw the trunk with two guards pass her looking for a parking spot. She laughed; it was so hot out she couldn't wait to feel the AC inside.

She scrolled through her iPhone as she walked with her head down, speeding as her heels clicked on the cement. Within seconds she heard a loud horn blow which made her look up and stop to see a Viper almost crushed her feet.

"Damn, just run me over!" she said, throwing her hands in the air as the driver rolled down his window.

***

Lil Ali was just coming from CNS. He didn't see the young woman in the green dress because she was moving so fast.

"I'm sorry, beautiful, I will never hit an angel," he said, admiring how beautiful she was

"While I hope we can meet again, maybe I should have let you hit me, sexy, see you around," she said, walking off with a sway in her sexy hips. She was shocked at how sexy he was. She never felt butterflies, and her panties were soaked.

Lil Ali saw two big Mexican men in suits trailing behind the young girl. He grabbed his draco. The men gave him an evil scary look and made their way in the salon behind the young woman. He spinned around the parking lot and looked at the black jeep license plate that read: "La Familia".

***

Ayesha was at a local park a block away from the house they were renting in a lower class neighborhood. Ayesha hadn't worked out in weeks due to so much stress but now she had to focus. She was running a park track on her sixty mile.

She ran hard in the heat, listening to her iPad—a DMX song. She had two miles left then she had to sprint, run the stairs, squats, lunges, jumping jacks and core exercises left. Exercising and praying was her only escape. She had plans to get her son and she wasn't leaving without him.

***

Winston-Salem, N.C.

Agent Camilla was bent over on her king-size bed, clutching her Dior sheets as her man—Lance—guided her hips to his deep thrusts. He slid his erection in her as she moaned, as he fucked her hard from behind.

"Ugghhh, shit, yes, papi, fuck that pussy!" she screamed, feeling his ten-inch snake ram in her tight pussy that was fit for his monster.

Seconds later she started shaking while letting out low groans that got louder as she climaxed with a scream. Before he cum, he pulled out so he could save the best for the last.

148

"I miss this dick," she said with her hair everywhere, giving her a wild sex look as she got on her back.

"I can tell with this wet pussy," he said as sweat dropped down his six-pack and chiseled chest while he slid the head of his dick against her tight hole. He slowly pumped in and out of her while she bit her lower lip, making a sour face as he tore her pussy up.

The sound of her wetness and moans filled the room as she started to fuck back.

"Ojj—shit—Uh'hh'l'h—fuck me!" she yelled at the top of her lungs as she came again. Lance tried to hold on as he went faster, rocking her body like a wave. Minutes later he came in her as his cum poured out her pussy as she pushed it out with her own.

"Damn!" Lance said, exhausted as he laid down next to her, drained from the three hours of fucking his lover. The two both had busy lives; him as a business owner and her as a full-time agent made bad timing for the couple who had been together for three years.

Lance was thirty-one years old, sexy, six-two, chocolate and Indian, big arms and chest plus a six-pack, clean cut, waves, and he was good in bed—every woman's pleasure. He did a four-year prison bid in the feds years ago for drug trafficking. When he came home, he opened an Auto Body shop and a clothing store in Greenville. He was originally from Brooklyn, NY but he had been in Carolina for years.

The two met at a comedy club and since then they were in love. She knew about his past life but she was okay with it because he changed for her.

"How's work, babe?" he asked as she played with his prison tattoos that covered his chiseled body.

"Okay, I guess, a lot going on but it will work out," she said in a strong Spanish accent.

"Good. I know they got the best of the best," he said, kissing her soft lips, climbing out the bed to see it was six and time for him to go open his shop in an hour.

"You hungry? I'ma make breakfast then take a shower. Feel free to join—better yet, don't. Can't let you open up the shop late again," she said, getting dressed as she chuckled because her pussy was sore but her mouth wasn't. She loved sucking his dick in the shower, feeling the hot water hit her hair while he banged her throat.

"Until later," she said, thinking about her caseload for tonight but she was still focused on the killing of all those elementary school kids. She wanted justice.

Chapter Twenty-Four

Medellin, Colombia

Rigo DeLos Guerrero sat by his outside pool smoking an expensive cigar on his forty-eight acres near the Pacific Ocean and between the Andes Mountains.

Rigo was the boss of the Guerrero Cartel family which was passed on by his father for over six decades. The family controlled the drug traffic and violence plus the government from Medellin, and Pasto and the capital Bogota. At sixty-two Rigo was in top shape even with lung issues from smoking cigars for years.

Medellin was the birthplace of "Los Hampois" (the Hoodlums) , the large organization that made millions in drug trafficking throughout America. During that era, the Guerrero Cartel was on the rise and they eventually took over the city.

For years the Guerrero family had the government under their authority which was the republics and the Supreme courts.

With being the most feared man in North America, he operated an army stronger than Hitler and his Nazi party.

The Colombian flag hung from a pole in the far end of his backyard; the flag was three horizontal bands of yellow top, double-width, blue, and red. Yellow is for the gold for the Colombia land; blue for the sea on it, and red for the blood spilled in attaining freedom.

Armed guards surrounded his palace with assault rifles just in case because the family was at war with two other cartel families.

Rigo sipped some of his tea, thinking about Ali's trip to the States and if he was safe because, after all, he was investing. Since his arrival in Colombia, Rigo took full advantage of becoming co-partners with Ali on his business investments within his casino.

He pushed a button on his remote for his beautiful maid to come out so he could prepare for his meeting in Venezuela with the Fernando Cartel.

"Yes, sir." A beautiful woman in her late twenties with blue eyes, long hair, and curves to die for walked out with a tray of cigars.

"Tell Manuel to get the team ready so we can take my jet to the meeting," he said in his smooth voice.

"Okay," she said, walking off in her heel showing her toned nice legs, as he looked in the mountains.

***

New Mexico

Lil Ali had been following the Jeep and the pretty girl for hours now. They were pulling into a gated mansion in an upper class neighborhood.

Lil Ali parked close to the estate, taking pictures of the guards, license plate, windows, every useful detail. A young woman from the shopping center made her way into the 2.9-million-dollar mansion, a man in a suit came walking out the house, with a gang of security.

He snapped pictures of the man kissing the girl on the cheeks as if he was her father. Lil Ali saw him climb in a Bentley followed by three GMC trucks. Lil Ali pulled out in reverse, not wanting to be seen as he raced down the street on his way back home to report to Ayesha.

***

Taqiq just got done making his prayer, and he climbed in his bed reading a children's book while eavesdropping on the commotion going on outside his door.

An older man walked in tucking a gun in his holster; the man wore cowboy boots and slacks with a Gucci button-up.

"I see you're enjoying this a little too much," Ole Bay stated as he sat on a small children's chair looking at Taqiq. Ole Bay had been watching the cameras in the room for a couple of hours and Taqiq seemed to be enjoying himself as if he was on a kid vacation.

Taqiq was silent. He just continued to read his book, paying Ole Bay no mind

"You can fucking play deaf if you want," Ole Bay said, snatching his book from his hands. "Listen, dear, you little bastard, I don't kill kids but now my wife and daughters are gone, I will love to put a bullet in your little head and bury your body in the woods," Ole Bay said.

"Sir, I'm only a kid. I have no clue what you are talking about. You killed all those kids, Mister?" Taqiq asked.

Ole Bay looked at him and slapped the taste out his mouth as he walked out the room, leaving the guards to attend to the kid as he went upstairs to meet Pedro.

***

Lil Ali walked into the new two-bedroom empty house that was filled with boxes. The neighborhood was basically filled with Mexicans and Natives.

"Hey, baby, how was your day?" she said, sitting on the living room couch eating sushi. "I ordered you Chinese food. I gotta go out and buy some pots and pans to cook tomorrow," she said in her Fendi sweatsuit with a fresh face that glowed from the cocoa butter she used on her skin.

"I'm good, mom, but I been busy doing some research and look what I just so happen to run into," he said, taking off his shoes, stepping on the fresh rug as he showed her the photos he took. "I don't know who they are but I know they connected. I can feel it. They move too strong," Lil Ali said as Ayesha scrolled through his pictures of the young girl, guards, the mansion and then she saw a familiar face as she stood up and walked to her laptop.

Ayesha did some typing as Lil Ali stood behind her, as she gave off a light smile. "Get ready for tonight," she said as she ran all the license plates to find one person connected to whoever these tycoons were.

***

Blanco was your average Joe who owned a loan company but he was also a financial advisor. He would take care of all of Pedro and his family finances from cars, home, trips, bills, anything, you name it; he was the family accountant.

He walked into his town house in the city of Alamogordo where he lived with his wife and son who was currently in Montana with family members. He had a long day at his loan office. He just wanted to sniff some coke and go to sleep. Being a full-blooded Mexican, working hard was in his bloodline but dealing with the Cartel was a headache, and he was ready to give in and move his family with him.

Once in his bedroom, he dropped his briefcase but before he even turned the lights on, he felt cold steel to his dome.

"This will be quick and easy—tell me about your boss," Ayesha said, sitting in a lazy boy chair as Lil Ali flicked on the lights with his free hand, with his pistol trained on his head.

Blanco's heart stopped. This was why he was scared to deal with the cartel but the money was amazing.

"I—I—I—" he stumbled over his words until Lil Ali cracked him in his head, knocking him on the floor as a small gash appeared.

"Okay, please don't hurt me. I work for his family. I handle all his business affairs," he said.

"Go grab every document you see. I got him," Ayesha said as she stood up dressed in all black with a pistol aimed at him, as Lil Ali ran off.

"I work for Pedro; he is a powerful man. I must warn you—he will kill everything you love," he said nervously.

"I don't want Pedro. I want his boss," she said.

"Ole Bay," he said as he froze. "I never saw him but I heard scary things about him but I know he is in New Mexico."

"I know but where can I find him? Your life depends on it," she stated as he put two and two together, knowing she had to be the one who killed Ole Bay family on the news.

"Found everything," Lil Ali said with stacks of papers in his hands.

"Guess we got everything we need," Ayesha said as she blew his brains out and told Lil Ali to drop off the documents and help her drag him to her trunk; she had a plan for him.

Chapter Twenty-Five

Phoenix, Arizona

Ole Bay was hiding out in his ranch-style house in the outskirt of Phoenix surrounded by horses, cows, and farmland. This was a place only few of his men knew about to keep his safe house private.

Hours ago his men informed him about Pedro's body being found chopped up into body parts in a hefty garbage outside of his capo gate

After thinking, he knew it was Ayesha who sent the nausea message to get his attention of course and he felt it; she was closing in on him

Pedro was angry when he spoke to him earlier; he thought this whole situation was a bad idea that could backfire but Ole Bay saw it from a different angle. He was sitting in his quiet room thinking of a new idea because time wasn't on his side.

***

New Mexico

Cattelina laid in the hotel bed exhausted from the long flight from North Carolina. She pieced up all the missing pieces to the puzzles; that's how she ended up here.

She knew of the whole situation between Ole Bay and her sister. If her sister was anything like her then she wouldn't stop at anything to get her son back.

After days of research she was able to track down Ole Bay and his organization here in New Mexico—his new turf.

Today was going to be a busy day for her. First, she needed a rental car to travel. She thought a bike would do, she loved sport bikes. Then second, she planned to hunt down one of Ole Bay associates that could lead her to Ayesha or her nephew because she knew the two were lurking. Then she had to go to a gunshop.

She climbed out the bed in a pink see-through lingerie set showing her perfect body as she walked barefooted to the bathroom. She brushed her teeth and fixed her hair, ready for her shower but she wished she brought her vibrator with her because she was a climax nympho but her pussy was deadly.

In a warm shower she let the peach Aloe soap raise off her smooth tight body, relieving herself while gathering her thoughts as she did for years as a quick meditation.

The thought of her killing Ayesha brought a wave over her body of sensual pleasure, but she understood she could also lose her life and she was okay with that. She got dressed without make-up and left the hotel room with a Birkin bag looking like a model.

***

Days Later

Trailing Mary for the last couple of days had been easy for Lil Ali. He was able to slip a GPS mag under her muffler when she was out on a date with a cute white chick and two boys a little older than them both—two African-Americans.

Lil Ali was four cars behind the SUV, following Mary through the mall's crowded parking lot. Everything was coming together. Ayesha found out that Pedro was the capo of Ole Bay and Mary was his daughter. She was finally closer to finding Taqiq, thanks to Blanco documents she took from his house.

Once he parked at the far end of the parking lot, he saw Mary get out of her Benz in a red sundress with her hair hanging down her back as the desert heat and the high humidity surrounded the city atmosphere.

He saw her walk through the Macy's entrance with two fat Mexican guards thirty feet behind her dressed in casual attire. Hopping out clean in his Balmain jeans, top, and Versace loafers with fresh two braids that hung down to his lower abs, he looked Spanish instead of black.

***

Mary walked through the mall like a diva, as if she owned it—which she could if she wanted it. She strolled through her favorite store which was the Celine designer store. Her closet was full of Celine clothes, heels, bags, and belts.

She saw her guards at the food cart through the glass window eating hamburger and fries as they always did when they came to the mall with her, as ordered by Pedro.

Mary saw new perfume next to the sunglasses. She loved perfumes and she always got a couple everytime she came in here, plus a new smell for her double date tonight with Melissa wouldn't hurt. Lately they have been double-dating with two black college basketball players three years older than them both.

While getting new fragrances, she walked down the aisle towards the Celine purses to see a familiar face looking at some jeans for men. When she got a better look at him through her designer shades, her heart started to race.

"Fuck!" she said loud, trying to hide behind a coat rack. She couldn't believe it's the kid from the parking lot; he had been on her mind since that day she told all her friends about him.

He was walking her way. She acted as if she was looking at the Peacoats, which was odd because New Mexico was hot all year around.

When the two saw each other, they made a strong eye contact and paused, both looking each other up and down. Lil Ali was wondering how thick and perfect her body was and felt himself getting aroused.

"Must be my lucky day, I guess the town is small," Lil Ali said, smiling, approaching her.

"I guess so, stranger, I see you got good taste," she said, looking at his red and blue Balmain outfit.

"Likewise," he said, looking at her Gucci sundress and Gucci belt wrapped around her small waist as her ass and curves stuck out like a sore thumb.

"What's your name anyway?" she asked, trying to stay calm as her hand got sweaty due to nervousness as he looked in her bright beautiful eyes.

"DeWayne. How about you, beautiful?" he said as she blushed hard.

"Mary. You must be new. I never saw you around here until recently," she said as they started to walk through the store side by side.

"I just moved here from Atlanta," he said with a quick lie.

"How old are you, DeWayne?" she said.

"Eighteen," he replied honestly.

She smiled and said, "Me too," as she picked up four Celine sunglasses worth $900 apiece, walking towards the cash register.

"You got a man because I'll hate to push up on a man's life support," he said as she laughed.

"No man but a crazy father and family—you know how Mexicans are," she said. "That has nothing to do with us or whatever we choose to do," she said, looking in his hazel eyes, letting him know she was down for whatever as he nodded.

"You get to the point," he stated.

"Only when I know what I want and how I want it," she said, grabbing his arm, stopping him then kissing his soft lips passionately as customers watched the two love birds, remembering when they were young.

"Uhmmm," he said as she pulled back, smiling.

"Take my number. I want to see you tonight. I got curfew but don't worry—sneaking out is my rehab," she said as she placed her number in his phone before paying for her items and walking out, leaving him watching her as she met up with the two guards.

***

Ayesha and Lil Ali were making salat on the living room carpet facing east as incense burned throughout the house.

"You make sure you are safe tonight. I been watching Pedro and his men closely but nothing useful that could lead me to my son," she said, standing up in her garment.

"I understand but we should just get Pedro, kill whoever in our way, get all the info we need from him. I'm sure he knows."

"This is chess—we move accurately. These men are wise and sharp; they will expect tactics of such. You gotta plan with time, I love you," she said, going to her room.

Romell Tukes

Chapter Twenty-Six

Lower East Side, NY

Face walked into the lobby of his fancy expensive condo, passing the security guards as he nodded. He just arrived from Maryland, B-More, after having a big meeting with his crew out there on the Westside and Cherry Hill.

The lower eastside was a business area and for upper class families but this was his low-key hideout. He also had a small house in Long Island and another condo downtown Brooklyn where he rarely stayed at.

Once in his luxurious condo, he tossed his keys to his Audi A8 on his marble and limestone countertop in his kitchen. The apartment was large with two bathrooms, glass showers, a Jacuzzi, a walk-in closet, a master bedroom, a fireplace, and a beautiful view of the Hudson River. The living room had a mini bar with stools, wall-to-wall carpet, flat screen TVs and surround sound system.

Face smelled a strong scent of Muslim oil which made him reach for his pistol, and he could feel someone was in his home.

"There's no need for that, Face, please I came in peace, brother," Ali said as Face turned on the lights to see him sitting peacefully in a Gucci suit with a low cut and shiny shoes with red bottoms.

"Nigga, who the fuck are you?" he demanded with 9mm pointed at Ali.

"Ali. We met years ago through Fatal—my pops and Havoc were like brothers," Ali said calmly.

"Man, what the fuck! I thought you were dead," Face said, confused, remembering Ali—the hood legend—as he finally lowered his gun.

"Yea, it's a long story but I faked a death to protect the one closest to me but I know you're busy so I won't take up too much of your time," Ali said as he stood up.

"I'm sorry about what happened. I heard the news but how the fuck did you get in my condo?" Face said, walking to his bar to pour a shot of liquor.

"Drink?" he asked.

"Nah, I don't sip but you need to tighten your security but the man who kidnapped my son is the same man who tried to kill me and failed but he is responsible for your father's death and that is why I'm here," Ali said as Face took a hard shot of dark Henny.

"So you think you can come to my city and try to muscle me or sweet talk me into *what* by using my father name leverage?" Face said, getting angry by his disrespect.

"I respect you as a man. You build a firm empire. I am going to get my son back regardless. I've been a ghost for ten years and I have no army no more. I just thought you would want your father's name to rest in peace once and for all, and two heads are better than one. I'll hate to waste anymore of your time. Here is my number if you come to a change of thought, brother," Ali said, laying a piece of paper on the glass table as he stood to leave while Face back faced him as he looked at the bright skyline.

"How I know you won't backstab me like how you did Fatal?" he asked softly.

"I only cross the double-cross. I live by morals. I'll be flying or driving to New Mexico in the morning. I'm staying at the Mar-riott—room two twenty-four," Ali said, walking out.

Face poured himself a drink as he heard the door closed. He threw his cup on the wall, watching it shatter, thinking about all the vows he made as a kid to one day find his father's killer. He sat on his couch as he closed his eyes and thought back to when he was a kid and his pops was alive over twenty years ago—Philly.

"Son, you see this shit, look around," Havoc said to Face as they stood in Havoc's trap house as naked black women bagged up coke and dope with masks and gloves on.

"I see, daddy," Face stated as he saw five big black males with AK-47 and big beards watching the door.

"This is the part of the game that comes with ease. A dummy can sell drugs to people but it take a wise man to get in and get the fuck out. You see I'm not so wise but I know you will be," Havoc said, rubbing his Muslim beard, walking into a small room full of bags of money and stacks of money all over the room as workers counted it all up.

Face nodded, knowing one day he was going to be just like his father—if not richer.

***

Lil Ali and Mary had been creeping around almost every night and she was star-stuck by him. This was their third date this week and Mary was ready to give him her all, and tonight was the night.

The Dodge minivan Lil Ali drove was parked in the parking lot overlooking the dark river as the stars and moon showed bright and clear.

"I'm so happy to be with you, papi, it feels so good to be with you," she said as she leaned in to kiss him as a Chris Brown album played in the background.

"I feel the same," Lil Ali replied, looking at her skin tight bodycon Prada dress that hugged her nice round breasts and showed her thick thighs.

"I think I'm in love with you," she said, waiting for a response.

"I'm falling for you too," he said, knowing his heart was only for Nicole who he missed dearly.

"I want you now, Ali, just let me—please!" she begged as she looked him in his soft eyes as she went for his Hermes belt, undoing it, as he leaned back with a hard-on as she licked her lips.

Mary pulled his hard large dick out and looked at him crazy, never seeing a dick so big. Her pussy was on fire.

She opened her warm wet mouth and began sucking his dick, slowly making love to it as it disappeared between her thick lips. Her head bobbed up and down in his lap as she spit on it while deep-throating as much as she could while he moaned as she speeded it up.

The slurping noises could be heard miles away as a thin line of pre-cum spun a thread in her mouth as she continued to give him a crazy blow job. He began to face-fuck her as she sucked faster as her thick lips stayed firm on his shaft as she took all of him down her throat. When he came in her throat, it was thick and creamy but she swallowed all of it.

"Damn, baby!" Lil Ali said, feeling as if he was on cloud nine.

Mary wiped her mouth as cum dripped from her chin, as she slid her thong off and lifted her bodycon dress while looking out the tints for police because they drove around every hour or so.

"Fuck me, DeWayne, please, I need to feel you," she said as he looked at her pretty phat shaved pussy that was dripping cum down her inner thighs. Lil Ali placed a condom on his dick and laid her down in the back as he climbed between her legs.

He slid his dick against her tight vaginal lips that was thin and smooth as he felt her juices while entering her

"Uhhmmm, shit, more!" she screamed as he slowly pumped, feeling her pussy walls grip his dick. Once he got deeper, he started to fuck the life outta her as she screamed and gasped for air as she felt multiple orgasms explode in her body.

Minutes later, after missionary position, she climbed on him and rode his dick like a cowgirl as she popped her firm curvy ass up and down on his dick until he filled her stomach.

After they both came, the two were sweaty, tired, exhausted and drained.

"If I ask you to do something, would you do it? And just know I never felt this way about no man except you," she said while getting undressed, still breathing hard, as her breasts popped out firmly at attention.

"Yea, of course," he said as he laid there naked on the blanket with all the back seat down as R&B played in the system, as the sweet smell of sex could be smelled heavily.

"Can you fuck me in my ass?" she said, handing him a small tube of KY jelly and got on her knees, bending over as her ass spread. Her pussy was poking out while her small asshole that was also clean shaved laid itself bare.

Lil Ali put some lube on his finger and played in her anus as he slid on another condom then he positioned himself, grabbing both of her ass cheeks. He was shocked at how phat her ass was. It looked as if she got ass shots as he slowly entered her back.

"Ug-g-g-h-h, fuck, it hurts but don't st-o-p-p-p!" she yelled as he got deeper in her tight ass. Her ass was so tight it was hurting his dick until she loosened up as she started throwing it back at him.

"Fuck me ass harder!" she yelled, backing her ass up harder on his dick as she cum out her pussy and ass.

"Ohhh yess!" she screamed as she double climaxed as he nutted in the condom. When he pulled out, she took off his condom and gave him another blowjob, almost making him cry then they fucked doggie-style.

Chapter Twenty-Seven

New Mexico

Cattolina was sitting behind the wheel of her parked rental car, watching the scene unfold in front of her own eyes. She was parked across the street from the med-size Mexican restaurant that was closed at eight in the morning.

The past week Cattolina had been watching Ramirez like a hawk. He was one of Ole Bay's top associates in his drug ring in the States. She knew he would lead her to Ayesha but right now she needed to find Ole Bay, and Ramirez was going help her.

She sipped on her Starbucks coffee, checking the time as a white Porsche Panamera pulled up in the parking lot across the street in Guya Uno restaurant.

"About time," Cattolina said as Ramirez hopped out to prepare to open the restaurant as he did every morning.

***

Ramirez Gonzalez Lopez walked up the stairs leading into his establishment. He was the first one here every two hours before he opened on Monday through Friday and the manager opened up on the weekends.

Ramirez was a full-blooded Mexican raised in the Mexican Cartel in Mexico but moved to the States to open a chain of Mexican restaurants for his people. He worked for Ole Bay as a hit-man and drug trafficker but now at the age of sixty he was mainly a business-man and taking care of his family.

Once inside, he placed the "We're closed" sign on the door and went to his office in the back of the kitchen to make some calls and count the gross income of the week.

***

Cattolina placed her Dolce & Gabbana shades over her face and added a little lip gloss to her full lips then climbed out the rental in a black Dior slit dress with a pair of pumps with strap laces.

She walked across the street with confidence as her heels clicked on the hot pavement as her coach purse hung around her frail shoulder while her breasts hung out on the side to tease and seduce who she chose.

Without any hesitation Cattolina slid a credit card in the slot of the glass door, trying to yank it open and within seconds she was inside. Once inside, the doorbell made two loud noises to alert employees of customers.

Inside was large with a stage, a bar, a food bar, tables and chairs on top of the wood tables, and the strong scent of Spanish food lingered in the air.

"Ms, excuse me, we're closed. How did you get in anyway?" Ramirez walked out from the back kitchen in a gray Brooks Brothers suit with a cleaning towel hanging from his shoulder as if he was cleaning or washing dishes.

"Oh no, I'm sorry. I'm not from around here. I was just very hungry. I've been driving for fourteen hours. I just needed some breakfast. I saw the door was unlocked so I just came inside. I'm sorry. I'll be on my way," she said as he looked at her perky breasts, curves, and flat stomach as well as her beauty.

"Hold on. I am making a special expectation for you as long as you enjoy breakfast with me. I should be done cooking within seconds. Have a seat please," he said, flipping a chair off as she walked towards him to sit.

"Okay, sounds like a plan," she said, sitting, crossing her legs, giving him a quick look of her thong and lower ass cheek as she leaned over giving him a glimpse.

Minutes later, Ramirez walked out with a tray with two plates full of food and two glasses of white wine to spice things up.

"Wow! Looks good," she said as she saw eggs, bacon, hash browns, steak wraps and spicy sauce.

"It is. I have many talents, young lady, but what is your name?" he asked, staring at her breasts while eating his food as she did the same.

"Katy," she said, slowly placing the large sausage in her mouth as his dick got hard.

"What's your business here if I may ask?" he stated in his strong Spanish voice, trying to figure out her distinguished accent.

"Good question. I was starting to assume you'll never ask, Ramirez Gonzalez," she said, surprising him she knew his name and he never informed her. "I'm here for you," she said as she swiftly pulled out a .44 Bulldog Mag and pointed it directly to his face, smiling.

"Wait, wait, I have money. Please take it and go. You have no clue who I am, Katy, so take the diner and go. I may spare you your lovely life," Ramirez said smoothly, still eating his breakfast wondering who set him up.

"I just need to get in touch with Ole Bay—that's why I'm here so give me his info," she said sternly.

Ramirez gave a short laugh. Listen, cutie, you barking up the wrong trees in the woods. I will—" Ramirez paused, thinking about the killer who murdered Ole Bay's family and looked back at her.

"You're the one," he said, leaning back, knowing he was fucked and he never carried guns.

"You have three seconds—one—two—"

"Okay, there, take it and go. I want nothing to come back to me," he said, writing down an address. Once she took the napkin with the address, she shot him in the face four times before picking up her wrap and eating it.

***

Ayesha just pulled into Gaya Uno Mexicana restaurant to only see a white Porsche parked in the lot. She knew Ramirez was a key player in Ole Bay's organization for over twenty years and it was easy to locate him. She only hoped he would be useful before she kills him.

She parked the minivan next to his Porsche and climbed out in a business suit, slacks and a blazer in hope to convince him that she is looking to invest in his chain of businesses.

As soon as the van doors closed, she checked her side, feeling her pistols while walking towards the restaurant. Within fifty feet of the restaurant she saw a woman wearing a dress and designer sunglasses walking down the stairs in heels as if she was a diva or model.

She wondered if she was an expensive hooker or a side girl, or even maybe his daughter as she grew closer.

"It's closed I believe," Cattolina said, walking past Ayesha, barely looking at her, thinking she was an investor and business saleswoman.

When Ayesha heard the Middle Eastern voice, chills went up her body as she stopped, feeling something was wrong. As soon as she turned around, a long barrel was pointed directly at her.

"Ayesha, you look the same as you do in your pictures," Cattolina said coldly.

"Thank you but you got the wrong bitch," Ayesha said as Cattolina took off her sunglasses as the morning breeze pushed her thin long hair to the side.

"Sorry, I wish but you're my sister. Hadrat told me a lot about you. She wanted us to meet before you killed her. She took good care of me," Cattolina said with emotion.

"Nice to finally meet you, sorry this way, but I'm a little busy as you see," Ayesha said, thinking about disarming her then killing her in the empty parking lot.

"You don't have to worry about Ramirez. I already took care of him. I came all the way from Dhabi to kill you, now I can kill two birds with one stone then for the bonus I kill my handsome nephews," she said, ready to get it over with.

"Leave me fucking kids alone but maybe another time we can meet and have coffee," Ayesha said as she slid a long blade out her sleeve and swung towards her neck but she was too fast as she ducked.

Cattolina saw Ayesha dash toward the van in zig-zag as she let off shots, shooting out the Porsche windows.

"You fucking bitch" Cattolina yelled as she reloaded as bullets flew past her head, as she ran for cover.

Ayesha was running towards her sister, shooting but Cattolina was extremely fast in heels as if she was a professional track star.

Chapter Twenty-Eight

Ole Bay slowly sipped his glass of Mexican Tequila while Pedro paced back and forth in his office thinking about all the murders that's been going on around his city.

"Pedro, we ain't had any issues for years and now it's like a storm flew in overnight," Ole Bay stated, taking a deep breath, lighting his cigar. The death of Ramirez and the police officer brought heat and unwanted attention to his empire.

"I don't really know what the fuck is going on but we have to find whoever is causing all this mayhem, boss, it bad for bussiness and what about the safety of our loved ones?" Pedro started thinking about his family while Ole Bay stared at a painting of the cartel boss, El Mayo.

"I know it's Ayesha but the other woman I truly have no knowledge of as of yet, but I gotta get rid of this. She is poisonous. I tried to hire to *asesinos* but when they heard her name, they never returned my fucking call but I promise I'll get it done before this goes any further," Ole Bay stated, blowing smoke out his noise.

"Okay, I have to go," Pedro said, walking out his office, passing a dozen guards in suits posted up in all quarters of the mansion.

Pedro climbed in his black McLaren 720S.

Cattolina shot back towards Ayesha, trying to hold her off but her sister was in beast mode, and a police cruiser pulling up caught her attention.

Both women saw the police cruiser and started shooting out the windows as the car crashed into a street pole and the officer died instantly. They both were out of bullets so they ran to their cars as more sirens could be heard within a block away.

They pulled off with their hearts racing, both mad they missed their targets—which was rare for them both.

***

With butterfly doors with two trucks following him out the long drive-way, life for Pedro was at its bottom. His wife served him with their divorce papers this morning but she agreed to stay in the house until Mary went off to college but their marriage was done.

Pedro drove home thinking about his family as the clouds formed dark gray as it began to rain hard, as he pushed the luxury car top speed down the wet highway hoping to crash as emotion overtook him.

***

Lil Ali and Mary leaned cuddled on the hood of his Viper at a local neighborhood park with a basketball court and playground. The two had been stuck to each other like glue. She was deeply in love with him. Tomorrow she planned to get his name on her left breast close to her heart. She couldn't wait. It was dark and humid outside tonight, so they both wore tank tops and Paris shorts worth five thousand apiece.

Mary laid between his legs thinking when she was going to be able to meet his family. He already met her best friends but her parents were another story. She also hadn't told him about her going off to college in a couple of weeks at UCLA.

"There is something I really need to speak to you about De-Wayne," she said, turning around, looking in his eyes with a serious look. "If that's even your real name," she added, crossing her arms as he gave her a blank facial expression.

"What are you talking about, Mary? Are you okay?" he asked, looking around as a couple of cars drove past the park on their way home.

"I know who you are, Ali Jr., and your mother Ayesha, the pretty woman who the cartels all fear," she said softly, looking at the worried look on his face. "I don't care about that, Ali, I love you and I'm willing to do anything to prove it to you," she said, putting her arms around his neck.

"How and when did you find out?" he said, angry inside she was two steps ahead of him.

"I'm no dummy, honey, you were too good to be true so I followed you one day and I saw Ayesha and the other day I sneaked into my father's office and saw pictures of her on his computer and you were in the top ten FBI Most Wanted."

"Damn!" he said, shaking his head as she kissed him.

"What are you really here for? Maybe I can help," she said in her sincere voice.

"Ole Bay," he said.

"My Godfather," she said sadly as his mind raced. "He is a powerful man, Ali, but lately I've been listening to his phone calls with my father and I never saw him so scared."

"Did they mention anything about a kidnapping because he have my little brother," Lil Ali said.

"No, the cartel don't kidnap kids. I'm sure of this, Ali. I was raised around this my whole life, but I heard nothing about a kidnapping and I'm so sorry to hear about your little brother," she said, feeling for her boo.

"I believe you," he said smoothly.

"But I can help if you want," she said, sounding willing to risk her life for him.

"Nah, I got this. Just tell me more about Ole Bay, baby, that will be enough," he said, holding her waist.

***

Mary went on for two hours telling him everything she knew about her Godfather. It was getting late and she needed to get home.

Lil Ali was ready to take her home. Now he got everything and some more from her about Ole Bay, he was pleased. The Viper pulled towards a dumpster next to a broken street light which made the end of the parking lot dark.

"I gotta take a piss real quick," he said.

"Okay and maybe I can suck your balls when you are done then deep-throat you until you cum in my mouth. I'm sure we have enough time," she said, climbing out the car behind him.

He pulled out his dick and pissed as she got undressed and looked around before she bent over; she always wanted to get fucked outside. Lil Ali saw her wide ass and phat pussy staring at him.

"I'll save this for last," she said as she rushed his dick and started to kiss it while licking his tip slowly then she went faster, making moaning noises as she deep-throated him while his pre-cum lingered on her tongue as she played with her pussy.

She was going crazy on his dick until he came; he almost fell over as he got weak in his knees as she cleaned his dick.

Once she was done, Lil Ali had a pistol pointed to her head as her life flashed before her eyes.

"I'm sorry, baby," he said.

"Don't. I love—" *Boom*! The loud blast from the cannon echoed through the lot as her naked body collapsed on the pavement as a big hole pierced her large forehead.

Lil Ali pulled his pants up and left her there, stepping over her blood. He had to hurry up and get home to inform his mom. It was only ten at night, so he still had time.

***

Ayesha was finishing up her night prayer when she heard the front door slam. Not expecting him back so early, she grabbed her sniper from behind her bedroom door and rushed out into the hallway barefooted in her garment to see her son pacing back and forth.

"What the hell is wrong with you? And take off your damn shoes," she said as she saw drops of blood freshly stained on her carpet.

"Mom, they know everything," he said, still pacing.

"Who? What are you talking about? Calm down and sit down," she said, turning off the tea boiling on the stove.

"I had to kill Mary. She knew my real name, about you, everything. Her father is on to us and she gave me all the info we'll need to find Ole Bay but—" she cut him off.

"Go get ready, we are going to pay Pedro a visit. Hurry, time is limited before they find the girl," she said as he walked off. "Where is she anyway?" she asked.

"I left her at the dumpster," he said as she shook her head, knowing the young generation had a lot to learn.

An Hour Later

Pedro woke up out of his sleep to use the restroom and go check on Mary, something he did every night. He looked over his shoulder to see his ex-wife sleeping peacefully as he slid into his Versace slippers as he climbed out the bed.

He walked down the marble hall to his daughter's room. Once in her room, he felt a strong breeze, seeing her window open which wasn't normal but it did get hot from time to time. Pedro saw his daughter laying under the covers. He smiled because she had a habit of sneaking out but lately she had been a good daughter.

He tiptoed through her room to close her window but was stopped dead in his tracks as Ayesha jumped out from under the sheets with a big pistol

"Where is my fucking daughter?" he asked as Lil Ali slowly creeped out the closet.

"Go clear the house and use the muffle; his men are near," Ayesha told her son who was dressed in all black just like her as he left the room.

"I ask the questions. Where is my son?" she asked.

"I don't know. The boss never told me and if he did, my loyalty remains with my cartel family," he said as she laughed before emptying her clip in his chest while her son walked in and told her he killed the wife in her sleep.

Romell Tukes

Chapter Twenty-Nine

It's been over seven days since Mary's body was found near a dumpster in a park across the street from a middle school. Two six graders smelled a strong foul odor on their way to school; so when they went towards the dumpster that morning, Mary's dead body had flies and mice surrounding her.

The news of Pedro and his wife also sparked the media attention when their security guards found them murdered that same morning.

Not only did the news hit the media hard, but it also hit Ole Bay—which made him more alert. He hadn't left his ranch since the news. Not only was he scared but he ran outta plans and he knew to go against Ayesha; he needed one fast.

He still had Taqiq in his safe house. He was thinking about just killing him and going back to Mexico because the feds were now lurking. He had the New Mexico border police under his belt because North Carolina agents were out of his control.

Ole Bay had no clue who the feds wanted or what, but he wasn't trying to get caught up in the web.

Today was Pedro and his family's funeral; he and his goons planned to pay their respect to the most trusted man in the cartel family. Ole Bay wore an all-black Tom Ford suit with shoes and a black diamond watch worth three million.

"Boss, the men are ready—they're all outside," one of his beefy guards said, standing at six-six weighing over three hundred pounds.

"Si, papi," Ole Bay said, sitting in his living room, smoking a Cuban cigar, inhaling the smoke.

***

The four black tinted GMC trucks were parked on the rocky driveway in a line as soldiers posted in front of the trucks.

Ole Bay walked out the house to smell cow shit which was the only thing he disliked about the country but besides that, today was a beautiful sunny day. He climbed in the second truck as two men climbed in the front following the first trucks; this way only to confuse his enemy because in times of war anything goes.

They drove down the empty country highway roads to see barns, farms, cows, chickens, and old rusty sheds.

Ole Bay heard a loud explosion which made him look back to see one of the SUVs blow up into flames, killing all four of his men.

"It's a fucking hit!" Ole Bay yelled as he heard another loud explosion, this time much closer, so close their truck almost swerved off the highway.

Ole Bay heard and saw a yellow Honda RX sport bike fly out of a small low-key dirt trail with two Mack 11's hanging from the biker's neck.

"Go! Go!" he yelled as the bike easily flew past him and the SUV in front of him as his heart raced. Ole Bay thought it was over until the biker stopped about 50 yards in front of them and did a donut racing back their way, shooting up the SUV in front of them.

"Kill that motherfucker," he shook the passenger while the other truck crashed into a mailbox. The passenger couldn't get a good range as he shot out the window at the biker as it got closer. The biker shot out the front windshield, hitting the passenger and driver both in the heart.

The SUV lost control and flipped over, leaving Ole Bay the only one alive. The impact of the flip made him black out for twenty seconds but when he came back to full consciousness, he saw the gunmen closing in on him. The biker wore skin-tight leather pants and high leather boots, all thanks to Givenchy.

Ole Bay was shaking like a stripper as he struggled to climb out the SUV with a few broken ribs and a numb spine

"Please take your time. I'm not here to kill you, that would have been too easy. I'm here to talk business," Cattolina said, taking off her helmet as her long hair dropped, as he stood up sweating and shocked, staring at her then his men.

"Come get on my bike—we have very little time before the police come," she said in her strong middle eastern voice.

"You killed my men and now you want to talk business. I should have you killed," he said as she walked off with her strut, smiling and laughing. Ole Bay heard sirens as she started her bike. He really had no choice but to get on because this was a messy situation he wanted no part of.

He climbed on her bike, holding her waist, smelling her strong perfume, trying to figure out what the fuck was going on because she wasn't Ayesha.

***

Once back at her hotel room, she threw her keys on the dresser as Ole Bay stood up waiting for an answer.

"Relax, grandpapi, why you look so sad? At least you're alive. I wasted air G74 gadgets I could have used for something else," she said, taking off her boots, showing her manicured pretty toes.

"Who are you? Enough with the fucking games!" he yelled.

"I'm Cattolina and I'm here to kill my sister, handsome, and you're going to help," she said as he quickly put two and two together; she was the other shooter from the restaurant he heard about.

"I don't need your help. I will kill Ayesha before I leave this earth and I'm not impressed with your work today. It gives me more reason not to trust you," he stated.

"Uhmm, okay, true but my sister will easily kill you and your army without breaking a sweat. You need me," she stated, looking at herself in the mirror while posing for a selfie for social media.

"You really have no choice," she said.

"You must not know who I am. So, how about you just leave my city alive, beautiful? You're too pretty to be buried in a dirt road," he said, making her laugh extremely hard.

"So funny. You lost your family. They are gone. your army is weak. I'm the best you got to get my sister, trust me now. Reason two—if you don't, I'll kill you," she said, pointing a gun with a red beam between his eyes, not smiling at all.

"Okay, your death wish but if you ever pull a gun on me again I'll kill you," he said.

"You have a way with words. My tight pussy is already soaking wet," she said, walking to her bathroom as he made a call for his men to come get him so he can still attend Pedro's funeral.

***

FBI, New Mexico

Agent Camilla and McKinnon been in New Mexico for a couple days hunting down Lil Ali and working on the new series of murders. She found out the cartel kidnapped Ali Jr's little brother. They found one of the gunmen from the elementary school shooting in Miami and he told it all.

Her and her partner knew something big was going on; that's why the murders of the city's most powerful men continued to build.

"Camilla, I just got the call," McKinnon said, rushing back into the subway restaurant where she was eating a healthy lunch as she always did.

"What now?" she said, eating her meal.

"Two cars exploded, two shot up, fourteen dead and guess who they work for—our guy Ole Bay," he said.

"Come on," she grabbed her FBI jacket and rushed out without paying.

***

Santa Fe, New Mexico

Ali and Face rented a big house with five bedrooms, three bathrooms, two acres, a pool and a guest house. They rented the place under a fake name to avoid any attention in the suburb area. They had over twenty goons there plus twenty more on their way driving, but they planned to stay in hotels for the weekend until the mission was complete at least.

Ali stood out back staring into the mountain tops and stars, thinking about his family. He been watching the news since he been here, and he knew the brutal murders were all Ayesha's work in the course of looking for his son.

"What popping, big dog? The rest of the crew just hit the city, so we all waiting on your call now," Face said, sipping a glass of Henny as his Gucci shades hung on his handsome face.

"Thank you once again. This will be over soon. I'ma go out and do some work. I got the drop on his location—one of his men work for Rigo; also he's his private eye," Ali said, glad to have Rigo at his aid because without him, he'll be wondering where to start looking.

"A'ight. I go shoot some C-Lo with the Danrv's son, hit me. I should be thinking you my father was a stand up nigga—I know he would have did this for me," Face said, walking off, leaving him in his thoughts.

Romell Tukes

Chapter Thirty

A Week Later

Cattolina stood on the small terrace inside her hotel room in a cotton robe, looking over the mountain tops and the colorful skyline.

Lately she been under Ole Bay and his army waiting for Ayesha to show up, but it seemed as if time was against her. Cattolina been holding a deep secret since she been in the States that very few knew about, which was the main reason why she was here. Thoughts made tears fall from her eyes everytime she thought about her horrible situation.

***

Years ago, Cattolina was dealing with an Arabian billionaire from Oman. The two got married and brought a daughter into the world. Months after their marriage, Cattolina murdered him and inherited his wealth.

She created her own army and empire with his blood money, but she was a success overnight. One night her daughter became sick with the flu and she was forced to take her to the nearest hospital in Dhabi.

Waiting in the hospital with four guards was no use for the twenty men that ambushed the hospital killing all of her men and kidnapping her sick daughter. Cattolina killed ten of the gunmen in a shoot-out that lasted thirty minutes in the hospital, killing fourteen innocent civilians as collateral damage in the process.

By the time she made it to the children care unit, her daughter was gone but there was a small note in the small size bed. She assumed it was retaliation for her husband's murder, considering he was a connected man.

She made it out of the hospital through the back entrance as police made their way in but the kidnappers were long gone.

When her team pulled up minutes later, she was so pissed and emotional she forgot the note in her pocket. She finally read it.

There was a name and number on it with an area code from Colombia but the name gave her chills; she knew the man they called Rigo was a very powerful man.

The night she called, she spoke to Rigo directly. He was very calm. He told her that her daughter was well taken care of and gave her an address in his city, Bogota, where she could meet him to speak.

The next day Cattolina arrived in Bogota alone. When she made it past the double steel gates, she saw over sixty guards surrounding the castle-like mansion with large assault rifles.

Once inside, she was searched twice because Rigo requested it; he knew Cattolina was a deadly dangerous woman. The guards escorted her to the large conference room Rigo held his business meetings in whenever he was in Bogota.

Inside the room there were expensive photos and paintings of classic warriors and Colombian presidents. At the end of the large cherry oak wood table she saw a handsome Latino man dressed in a tailor made suit playing with a laptop monitor built into his table for close surveillance.

"Ms. Cattolina, nice to finally meet you. Have a seat. You look amazing," he said, looking at her Versace dress that hugged her perfect breasts and curves.

"Where is my daughter? I've done nothing in your country," she said, still standing. Rigo pushed a couple of buttons and pointed to his monitor on his wall. The monitor showed her daughter in a small pink room sleeping in a baby carriage under a cartoon blanket which brought ease to her heart.

"What do you want?" she said with tears in her eyes, ready to kill.

"I'm Rigo and you will help me get your sister back. You have a lot at risk as you see, beautiful, but she is well taken care of. Now Ayesha killed my loved ones and bloodline. I want her. The only reason you're not dead is because I need you. I have her location but it's on you. Okay?" She slowly nodded.

**

Cattolina hated to reflect on that moment when Rigo threw a curve ball in her life; even though she hated her sister, she had better shit to do than play out nice with her. She walked back in her room and went to sleep thinking about her daughter's well-being.

***

Ali and Face sat in one of the two U-Haul trucks full of goons in the back, loading up their weapons, driving up Ole Bay's block.

The last couple of days Ali had been tailing Ole Bay closely, thanks to his inside guy, and today was the big day. Ali and Face's plan was to kill everybody in sight and get his son back. The trucks slowly rolled up Ole Bay driveway to be greeted by seven guards patrolling the driveway.

***

Guards walked around the driveway as two Rolls Royce Ghosts, Lambos, and Ferraris, filled the garages belonging to Ole Bay. The guards approached the trucks wondering what was going on because they were unaware Ole Bay was planning to move anything today.

"Excuse me, sir, are you sure you have the correct address?" the guards asked as they approached both trucks.

The back of the trucks doors slid open at the same time quietly as a gang of men hopped out of both in broad daylight dressed in all black with masks on and all type of machine guns

Rat-tat-tat! Bloc! Klick! Bloc! Bloc! Tat! Tat! The gunmen turned the Mexicans to Swiss cheese as they ran in the mansion like wild lost animals.

***

Ole Bay just got out the shower to be greeted by the two naked underage Spanish prostitutes flat-chested with small petite frame with deep pussys at only sixteen.

Ole Bay was ready for seconds on both women until he heard gunfire inside of his house which made the girls jump as he ran to his TV cameras. When he saw what was going on, he grabbed a vest and an AK-47, running out the room into a side door that connected to another room, leaving the girls screaming and crying.

Years ago, before he bought the house, he had extra rooms, a tunnel leading to the streets, and a safe room built inside for times like this.

Ole Bay had to get downstairs, and the only way was getting into the hallway but the gun battle between his men and the gunmen was like World War II outside the room, so he waited.

***

Ali was shooting his way downstairs with his assault rifle, stepping over dead Mexicans. The plan was for Ali to hit the basement where he heard Taqiq was being held while Face took upstairs.

Once in the basement, three guards hopped out from behind two sidewalls busting, hitting Ali in his shoulder as he shot one in his head. The other two shooters' bodies dropped as the goons riddled their frame with bullets.

"Ali, we see him!" one of the Blood yelled as he searched the basement while Ali got off the floor holding his bloody shoulder.

Within seconds they escorted Taqiq out the small cave to Ali. When Taqiq saw Ali, he froze because he looked just like him and his brother. Ali rushed to give him a hug, squeezing him to death.

"Who are you? My mommy sent you?" Taqiq asked as Ali's eyes got glossy.

"I'm your father," Ali said as Taqiq jumped in his arms, hugging him, this time hurting his shoulder.

"Take him out to the truck now. I gotta find this bastard," Ali said as six of his men took Taqiq upstairs, surrounding him because there was still a lot of shooting going on upstairs.

***

Ole Bay saw all of his men drop like flies out the crack of his door, but when he saw Ali's face walking up the stairs, his heart stopped. He thought he killed him. He couldn't believe what he was seeing as he kicked in every door looking for him; there was only one way out.

Once he heard the two shots killing the underage girls next door, he dashed into his hallway, making a run for downstairs while all the gunmen were posted upstairs.

When they saw Ole Bay, it was too late; he hit two of them with lucky shots as he ran for the elevator. Bullets grazed him, shooting past his head.

Face held Bare's dead body as Ali raced after Ole Bay who hopped in a small elevator leading into the basement. Ali ran to the basement to only see Ole Bay was gone; there was a built-in cave in the floor covered by a wood door. Ali was pissed but he told Face it was time to roll before the police came.

Romell Tukes

Chapter Thirty-One

Dexter, New Mexico

Ayesha sat at the waterfront near a train station in deep meditation, feeling relaxed, trying to get her thoughts together as the sun blinded her sight. It was ninety-seven degrees out and she wore her full garment and hijab. She just came from Jummah service.

Her mind couldn't shake the news she saw on Fox the other day when the police found over thirty dead bodies: most Mexicans and some African-Americans. What really caught her attention was: the mansion was less than ten minutes away from her house on a highway. The icing on the cake was when a picture of Ole Bay's face popped up on the news because he was wanted for questioning.

The news confused her as to who was the gunman to go against Ole Bay's crew and where her son was. Those were the questions she couldn't get out of her head; now she felt as if she was starting from the beginning.

Ayesha felt someone had been watching her closely since she left Jummah; she wasn't sure, that's why she was here. It was early afternoon, and civilians walked the park while some watched their kids play on the small swags and monkey bars on the playground.

Feeling as if someone was closing in on her from behind, she stood up slowly and with a swift one motion she leaped to her left side, stepping with a pistol directly at the intruder, about to shoot.

"It's me, it's okay, put it down. The police are in the next lot," Ali said as Ayesha looked at him as if he wasn't real with her gun still trained on him.

"No, no, no, no can't be—" she mumbled as the man that played in her dreams and mind approached her, looking like a clear cut lawyer in his Armani Exchange suit and Dior perfume with Gucci glasses on his smooth, still youthful face.

"I'm sorry. I had to protect you and our family—they would have killed you," he said, wiping her tears.

"They took our baby," she stated, sobbing on his muscular chest as he held her.

"I got our baby back. He's safe waiting for you," he said as she couldn't believe what she heard.

"Oh my God! That was you. Thank you. I miss you so much!" she said in her soft sweet voice.

"Thank Allah but we have to go. I want to see my other son and the feds are all over," he said, taking her hand, walking her towards the parking lot.

***

Lil Ali was exercising, running the track across the street from a local high school. He was on his seventeenth lap, running at a steady pace in his Under Armour tracksuit. Lately, he'd been so focused on finding his brother. Training wasn't even on his mind but he knew it was mandatory to build up his speed and endurance so he could withstand hardship at all times.

When he finished, he went to grab his water bottle near the water fountain as females ran past him looking at him sexually. Lil Ali dropped down and did two hundred burpees, squats, sit-ups and sprints in less than thirty minutes, finishing off his cardio session.

By the time he made it to his car, he saw a piece of paper on his windshield with a name and number. He ripped it up and tossed it out. The only woman he wanted was Nicole; he thought about her daily but he knew the feds were on him so he gave her space until he felt the time was right. Not hearing from her crushed his heart but he knew he had to focus because his and his baby brother's life was on the line.

He grabbed his tracfone off his car charge; he changed his phone every week so the feds wouldn't pick up on him. It was for emergency use only. He saw his three missed calls from his mother so he called her back.

"Hurry home. Allah has blessed us," his mom said as soon as she picked, as he heard his little brother's voice in the background with others.

"Put him on," Lil Ali said with watery eyes.

"As-Salam-alaikum, brother, I miss you a lot. Guess who is here," Taqiq said in his kiddish voice.

"Walaikum-salam," Lil Ali said, choking on his voice "I'ma see you when I get there, I love you!" he said, trying not to let his brother hear him cry as he hung up and pulled his draco from under his seat on to his lap.

***

Once he pulled into his mom's driveway, he saw four all- black trucks with tints and niggas standing around as if they were down with Malcom X and the F.B.I. He slid his two desert eagles in his holsters as he exited his car; the goons all nodded at him. Lil Ali could tell they were from New York—from their accents as they talked to each other in the driveway.

Inside he saw Ayesha sitting on the couch with Taqiq with a couple of men in the house, but the two men he saw in the kitchen caught his attention. When the man wearing a suit turned around to look at Lil Ali, his heart stopped. He could recognize his father in the dark. Lil Ali ain't know how to feel as the house got quiet, as he rushed upstairs to his room slamming the door.

"I got it, Ayesha, I have to explain myself," Ali said as he saw her about to walk upstairs.

"Okay," she said, going back to cater to Taqiq as he was telling her everything that took place.

***

Ali knocked on his son's door before walking inside to see him staring out his window with his back towards his pops.

"I know how you feel and you have the right to, but I lived a dangerous life and all of your lives were at risk so I had to be smart. Sorry I didn't come sooner. Every kid needs a father but you turned out good," he said.

"Man, that's your excuse, dawg, you played us and left us for dead. Family don't do that," Lil Ali replied.

"I understand but as a man I did what needed to be done. We are all still alive and well," Ali said as Lil Ali turned around to face his father.

"You brought Taqiq back. I respect that but my life is ruined now. I'm a wanted man," he said.

"Don't worry about that. I'ma take care of that after I take care of Ole Bay once and for all. I'ma send you and your brother to Philly until this is all over. Trust me—we will move as one now," Ali said as his son nodded.

"When we leaving?" Lil Ali asked.

"Midnight, son, just be ready," Ali said, turning to leave.

"Pops, just want to let you know I love you," he said seriously.

"I love you more," Ali said, looking at the younger version of him before leaving his son to think.

***

North Carolina

A Week Later

Agent Camilla's boss called her to his office to talk to her as soon as she got in the building; she had a long night going over reports and bias.

"Hey, boss," she stated as she entered her boss's office in her suit and blazer.

"Sit down," her boss said with a cold sharp tone as if she was a kid in trouble at school. "Listen, Camilla, you're a good agent, one of my best but this case you been working on is out of your league so that's why I'm snatching the case from you. Another department will take it. This isn't my decision, it's from the higher power. You and McKinnon should be suspended for going out of our jurisdiction but I stuck my neck out for y'all, so consider this a warning. Do I make myself clear?" he said firmly.

"Yes, sir, clear. Are we done?" she said, pissed off; he snatched the biggest case of her career.

"Done," he replied as she stood to leave.

***

Lance was in Camilla's apartment cooking her pasta and fried chicken with fish steak, which was one of her favorite meals.

"I can't believe this shit, baby, all my hard work—I almost had this case cracked wide open!" Camilla said, sitting at her diner table, talking non-stop as he brought her a plate and a glass of wine.

"Baby, chill, it's okay, relax. It's not always about work," he said, smiling as she began to eat her meal.

"Ummm—good!" she said, showing her dimples, licking her juicy lips the tomato paste on the corner of mouth.

"Glad you like it, enjoy your last meal!" Lance told her in a creepy voice which caught her attention, looking up at him to see him pointing a 357 mag directly at her face.

"Lance, what the fuck are you doing!" she said as he caught her off guard as her heart raced.

"Camilla, Camilla, Camilla, you should mind your own business but you gotta be superwoman, now look!" Lance yelled.

"Lance, what the fuck are you talking about?" she said, thinking how can she get to her work gun in her bedroom without dying.

"Are you that dick-drunk, bitch? I been selling drugs forever. I'ma street nigga, I even got my own set out here. I know you see my dawg paws, bitch, I'ma real Blood!" he said, showing her three dots on his right upper arm. "Where you fucked up at is with this case. The New York dude Face you was pillow-talking about is my connect and big homie, and he wants you dead. Sorry, still love you and you got the best pussy I ever had," he said as she had tears falling in her food.

"So I guess you was chasing clout and fame. I don't know why I couldn't see it," she said, mad at herself because she always had a feeling he was gang affiliated because of his tattoos, but she didn't want to press him or run him off.

"Call it what you want," he said, laughing.

"I guess I will see you soon," she said as he shot her twice in the side of her head, then running out the apartment with his hoodie over his face.

Chapter Thirty-Two

Santa Fe, NM

The last couple of days had been a vicious manhunt for Ole Bay all around New Mexico but Ayesha and Ali came up everytime. Tonight was the first night the two were together alone since the kids went to Philly under the supervision of a close friend of Ali.

The couple was staying at one of the finest hotels in the state in the penthouse suite which had an upstairs and downstairs, fancy wallpaper and carpeting, two Jacuzzis—one in the master bathroom and the other in the living room connected to a window overlooking the city.

"I always had a strong feeling you were still out there because I know you're too smart to walk into a trap unprepared," Ayesha said, sitting on the mink sheet in her Fending mini dress with a pair of heels on , showing lots of skin. Tonight Ayesha looked like a model straight off the runway while Ali looked the same in a white Micheal Kors button-up and slacks.

"I know but now it's all about the future, hopeful after I see Rigo I can go back to a regular life and run the casinos and raise my boys," he said as he took a seat next to his wife, rubbing her nice toned smooth legs, looking at the fireplace.

"I don't know if we will ever be regular but you will always be the love of my life and we will always be a family," she said, kissing his soft lips as his hands went up her white dress to feel her bare soaked phat pussy underneath her thong.

"Wait—I want to taste you," she said, stopping him as she stood up taking off her dress, exposing her firm perky breasts and clean shaved pussy. Ali took off his clothes as well, showing his defined body and chiseled six-pack he worked hard for.

"You're so beautiful," he said, looking at her amazing perfect body as she saddled herself between his legs to see his massive hard dick she missed.

She grabbed his penis and kissed it while stroking it as she spit on it. She wrapped her full wet lips around the tip and slowly traced her long tongue around it like a snow cone or ice cream cone, then she sucked it.

"Uhmmm—damn, baby!" he said, moaning, feeling her warm mouth gain in speed as she went a little deeper with a rhythm as her saliva coated his dick, as she relaxed her throat. She wasted no time in caressing him softly as he thrusted his hips while she went deeper up and down on his dick until she felt him down in her stomach.

Ayesha eagerly sucked his dick at a fast speed while pre-cum and spit soaked the sheets as she gave sloppy head. After ten more minutes of slurping noises and deep throating, he finally busted a big thick load in her mouth as she swallowed every drop.

"Damn! I should die more often," he said. She sat up wiping her mouth, laughing at how he was moaning like a little girl.

"Yeah, I bet. Now lay down so I can ride that dick," she said as her pussy was begging for attention.

Once he was able to get himself in her super tight pussy, she started riding his dick like a cowgirl as he grabbed her waist and pounded her pussy out as she screamed and climaxed.

After she came twice, Ali fucked her doggie-style as her yells could wake up the whole hotel. The two fucked until sun up, making passionate love.

***

The next morning Ali woke up in bed on an empty stomach to look to his left to see Ayesha gone. He jumped up naked and grabbed his fully loaded pistol on his dresser in danger mode until he smelled halal food being cooked.

He calmed down, took a deep breath and got dressed as the sun brightened up the room, making it a little warm. Ali brushed his teeth and took a piss, realizing his dick and body was sore from the long night of rough sex.

"Good morning, As-salaam-alaikum," Ayesha stated, wearing her Fendi lingerie, cooking with her ass hanging out the bottom which jiggled everytime she moved.

"Wa-alaikum-salaam. I smell you, beautiful," Ali said, hugging her from behind smelling the Dove soap on her soft skin. He loved that his wife was always clean and smelled good.

"Sit down and stop being nasty," she said playfully as he grabbed her soft ass with both hands

"I can never get enough of you," he said, sitting at the glass table in the kitchen area as she brought two plates of food behind him.

"We'll see if you can stand on that after breakfast but I spoke to the kids earlier. They're good. Abdul is fine and so is Lil Ali," she said, eating her eggs and halal veggie pattie.

"Good. Abdul is our best choice of trust at this point but we gotta find Ole Bay. My inside help came up missing so we got to find a new route." Ali noticed her nipple was exposed.

"I agree," she said, breathing hard, thinking about Cattolina.

"This week I will have to go back to Colombia to see Rigo but I owe him for his help," he said, eating his grits as Ayesha stopped eating and stared at him.

When Ali mentioned his name before, she didn't really think on it until now when it hit her

"Rigo?" she asked, trying to piece the puzzle together.

"Yea, Rigo Guerrero," Ali stated as food flew out of his mouth.

"The Guerrero Cartel, Ali!" she shouted, surprised as he looked at her, wondering what her issue was.

"You know him?" he asked, confused because Rigo claimed to not know Ayesha when he mentioned her.

"Too well, too well," she said, looking at her lover awkwardly, wondering if it was a hit on her life but she trusted him. "I killed his son and nephew plus a couple of more members in his family years ago. My father sent me on a mission," she said with her arms crossed.

"Fuck! I know something was wrong!" he shouted, angry, feeling as if Rigo set him up so he could get to Ayesha somehow.

"I'm sorry, Ali, but he knows who I am and he wants me dead," she said.

"I got a plan. I'ma handle him personally but right now you focus on Ole Bay and Cattolina," he said, standing up, leaving, walking to the shower.

***

Bogota, Colombia

Rigo was in his library inside of his ten-bedroom, six- bathroom, 6175 square foot mansion, playing chess with himself as a second person.

Guards surrounded his 15.4-million-dollar home 24/7, armed and ready just in case another cartel family wanted a war which many did with the boss of all bosses.

"Boss, we got a message from Ali. He says he will be back within a couple of days," one of his giant guards said as he entered his double doors. Rigo smiled and nodded, knowing a pup will always find his way home.

Rigo had big plans with Ali to take over American casino operations then kill him and of course his wife who was responsible for his loved ones' death over a beef with Abu Hurayra.

After he won his chess game, he walked in a door attached to another room full of pink wall paper and dolls to see Cattolina's daughter being fed by one of the house maids. He hadn't heard from Cattolina, but he would give her a couple of days or she would pay for it dearly.

***

Washington Heights, NY

Face pulled up to a nice low-key build in his GLK Benz to meet with two women he met the other night, both Latina beauties.

It was eleven at night and the block was dead, which was unlike the Heights which was 85% Spanish. Face parked behind a

BMW and walked in build 151 on Post and Academy. He took the stairs to the sixth floor and knocked on the sisters' door.

Angel opened the door wearing a bra and panties, showing her wide hips and double D breasts with a couple of tatts plus green eyes and tan skin.

"Hi, papi, come in," she said, smiling, licking her lips, turning around so he could see her ass bounce with every strut.

"Damn, mami, this how you gonna do me?" Face said, grabbing his dick in his G-star jeans as he followed her to the back of the dim apartment which was clean and neat.

"Me and me sister can't wait to fuck you, papi," Angel said, walking into a room to see her sister sitting on the bed playing with her pussy as he got a hard-on. Angel got on her knees, pulled out his dick and started to suck it in the doorway. Face was so caught up he didn't see the shadow behind him until it was too late; a masked gunman fired five shots in his head and ran out. The two Mexican women worked for Pedro. They were mules for him before he was murdered.

Romell Tukes

Chapter Thirty-Three

Phoenix, Arizona

Cattolina was bent over naked doggie-style, gripping the silk white sheets as she looked at her sex faces in the mirror while Ole Bay fucked her from behind in the fancy hotel room.

"Damn, you tight—Ugghh!" Ole Bay groaned while holding her petite waist steady as he struck in and out her tight walls. "I'm cumming!" he shouted as he pulled out, shooting a load on her nice round plump ass while she looked back at him.

Last night was a long night. Ole Bay sucked her pussy for hours, making her climax five times. His dick game wasn't all that, but six inches was enough for her tight pussy that will make any man go crazy. She also sucked his dick in front of his guards, almost making him cry. Her head game was good.

Cattolina kept him close and he did the same. He knew Arizona was a good hideout until he came up with a plan to get back across the border, a wanted man.

"You know, Cat, we should go to Mexico or Peru. My people will take good care of us. The feds are still scooping around but I have connections with powerful people in the field, but my main worry is Ali and Ayesha. Those two together will cause a lot of bloodshed!" he stated as they laid side by side in the king-size bed.

"You can leave as you please. Just because we fucked doesn't mean have a GPS on you. I have to find my sister. Ali's the person I care little about but I do need some men to help me," she said, sitting up, getting herself dressed.

"Oh no—you don't understand, Cat, she alone will kill the rest of my men. I can't afford any more losses. I killed Ali with my own eyes, and he is back. This man is very powerful just like his men-tor—Musa. You have no clue what you're dealing with." Ole Bay was getting dressed as well in his cowboy boots.

"Seems to me someone is scared of the boogieman," she said, playing while strapping up her lace Chanel heels.

"You should be. That's why I'm getting the fuck out of here today and you have a choice to come or die a slow death at that!" he said, putting his pistols in his side.

"I'm staying. I'll meet you after but I need some men," she said.

Laughing, Ole Bay replied, "My men are not your shield." He saw how sexy she looked in her Chanel dress, getting horny.

"Okay, love, keep your men, you have no clue who I am. I'm sure we'll meet again," she stated as she walked out the room with her sexy strut.

Ole Bay watched her speed away from the hotel in a white Audi A4 2.0, shaking his head.

***

North Carolina

It was early in the morning. The sun was still rising to its peak as Lil Ali did seventy down the highway. He had a new ID, new social security card, and license with a new identity just in case for some reason he was still wanted.

He was supposed to be in Philly with his little brother and Abdul, but he had to come check on Nicole. He tried everything to get in touch with her but he couldn't. He hoped she didn't move on with her life because she was the only person he wanted to be with. He knew now that everything was about over, things could go to normal since he wasn't wanted for the murders no more; it was a cold case.

He still wore a Jamaican hat with fake dreads to trick people as he leaned back in the all-black Cadillac OTS-V with the black tints Abdul let him use. Lil Ali thought it would be smart to go to Nicole's school first because on Monday mornings she usually always prepared for classes. After Nicole's visit, he had plans to go pay Bundles' mom a visit in Southgate to send him a strong message.

***

FSU

Forty minutes later he pulled the Cadillac into the large parking lot on the campus, hoping to see Nicole's black Kia in her parking spot, but instead he saw a red Mazda.

Lil Ali parked next to the sedan and followed the crowds of students onto the school's grounds towards her dorm lobby. Before he made it inside her building, he saw her neighbor walk out—a young cute Puerto Rican chick from the Bronx.

"Excuse me, is Nicole upstairs?" he asked her, stopping her in her tracks as she looked at him with an awkward facial expression.

"You have not heard? She was murdered a couple of months ago. It was big all over the school. Hold up, you look familiar. Oh shit! You were her—" was all she could say before he walked off leaving her standing there.

He rushed back to his car crying. He knew it was true because she was always reachable. Lil Ali googled her and saw her memory photos and rest-in-peace date with the details of her murder. He cried for ten minutes before pulling off on his way to Southgate.

Southgate, Fort Bragg

Lil Ali drove through the back entrance so nobody could see him. It was still early, so the hood was a ghost town. He pulled up next to Bundles' mom's trailer to see it was dirty as usual with old mattresses in the front infested with bedbugs, old broken toilets, sinks, and bikes

He placed a silencer on the tip of his pistol then he exited the car, thinking about Nicole.

***

Bundles' mom was on her knees in her living room giving a yang dope dealer a blowjob while her daughter was in the backroom waiting for school.

She was twisting her head on his dick while sucking it for dear life; she was coming up and down, deep-throating him while she spit on it

"Suck that dick," he said, as she made loud slurping noises. Her thick lips worked his tip as she looked him in his eyes as he couldn't hold on any longer. After he nutted in her mouth, he gave her two rocks while pulling up his baggy jeans, smiling because she had the best head in the hood, but her pussy smelled like shark meat.

She snatched the crack and shoved it in her bra as she heard her doorbell ring twice.

"Who the fuck is that? Wait right there, BJ," she said as she went to open her door to see a Jamaican man standing outside her door.

"What the fuck do you want and who are—*Psst! Psst! Psst!*" The bullet ripped through her skull, cutting her sentence short as her body dropped.

BJ hopped up with his pistol he always carried, but Lil Ali shot him four times in his heart, making him collapse on the couch choking to death on his own blood.

"Mommy," Teyana said as she walked out her room in her school uniform and Dora the Explorer backpack, ready for school to tell her mom she was late for school until she saw the dead bodies and gunmen.

"Ali," she said in her soft voice that became raspy with fear as she saw her mom dead by the front door. She recognized Ali with ease from being around him so much. Ali looked at her and paused, wishing she would have stayed in the room because now he was left no choice. He shot the little girl in the head and rushed out the trailer.

Once back in his car, he drove far away from Southgate and went to get some gas and some fresh flowers for Nicole's grave he was on his way to visit.

Chapter Thirty-Four

Cumberland Jail, N.C

Bundles sat in his cold cement cell in solitary confinement, staring at the slot on his metal door, trying not to move due to the restraints on his ankles and wrists.

Yesterday the chapel called him to his office to deliver him the news of the deaths of his mother and lil' sister. Bundles went crazy in front of the pastor, who had to call the team to restrain him as he got out of control. Since then he had been in the box crying for his lost ones.

Last week he made a deal with the government to cop-out to twenty years in federal prison after signing a 5K2.1 snitch agreement. The DA claimed it was the best deal he was going to receive because not only was Lil Ali's case dropped at the moment, but there wasn't enough solid evidence to build a firm case on him anyway.

Word also got out around the jail that Bundles was a rat so he'd been l on PC for months, plus he had a lot of enemies lurking around the jail waiting to catch him from things he did prior.

Bundles worked out everyday to keep himself mentally sharp. He would do two thousand push-ups and five hundred burpees for his wind before he came to the box.

He heard keys coming down the tier slowly as inmates started yelling and shooting as the young black female C.O. strut down the tier with mail in her hands.

She stopped at Bundles door and slid a piece of mail under his door and continued to pass the rest out, leaving her strong perfume scent on the tier for the inmates to lust over.

Without hesitation he slowly walked to his door as his wrist and ankles were extremely swollen. Once he finally got the letter, he opened it to realize there was no sender name; only an address which was his mom's address. His mind started to spin as he read the short letter.

Death Before Dishonor, my friend, how does it feel to be betrayed, rat? I'm sure your loss will cause grief. It's a shame. until next time. Your friend—

Bundles felt rage as tears rolled down his face. Ali killed his family. He should have known but he thought he was on the run. After an hour of crying, he placed a piece of paper outside the edge of his door, requesting the phone so he could call his lawyer to inform him of his family's murders.

***

FBI, N.C.

Agent McKinnon sat at his desk thinking about the call he just received from the public defender office. He was told the two murders in Southgate recently was retaliation for Bundles ratting out Ali. When McKinnon questioned how accurate the information was, the lawyer told him his client received a personal letter from him admitting to his wrongdoing.

Since the death of Camilla, his life had been upside down; he missed the young talented girl who was very witty and smart. Her death was still unsolved; her killer left no trace whatsoever and no witnesses. She kept her personal life to herself so Agent McKinnon was unaware of any friends or sexual relationships.

He grabbed his car keys on his way to the jail. If he had something, he could open back up this Ali Jr. case and nail him; he had a strong feeling about him.

***

Bogota, Colombia

Rigo sat in his backyard looking over the mountains, puffing on his expensive cigars, smiling to himself because Ali was minutes away from his castle and he had good news for him.

He had a strong feeling today was the day Ali would cut him in on his profits with the casinos and lead him to Ayesha's whereabouts then he could kill him.

Cattolina was still nowhere to be found but her daughter was still alive. Things were going too well to worry about her; he knew he'll handle her later.

Rigo heard the guards say the limo was pulling through the gates. He smiled and rubbed his smooth hands together.

***

Ali walked up the stairs, passing the lion statues in his European tailor-made suit looking like money, with a clean cut and an AP diamond watch.

There weren't many guards surrounding the entrance today as all eleven big Spanish men greeted him like he was family. Ali walked through the dining room toward the large marble floor kitchen to get to the backyard.

He stopped when he saw the beautiful maid he had an affair with for years; she was still deeply in love with him. When she got pregnant, nobody knew it was by Ali until the baby died of the flu and their love affair ended. She was born and raised a trained killer. At thirty years old she looked eighteen with a beautiful clear face, soft colorful eyes, petite but curvy, and with great sex appeal.

"Hey," she said softly as he broke their eye contact, and she continued to chop up greens and tomatoes for tonight's big meal as Rigo requested.

Ali always admired her beauty and strength. She told him her whole life story from how she grew up poor and saw the cartel kill her whole family and sell her off into the sex slave trade at nine years old. As she got older she was bought by a Colombian who never touched her sexually; he trained her to be an assassin—and that she was. When her mentor died of lung cancer, she came to work for Rigo who only kept her around for her looks but nothing sexually.

"I know we moved on but you saved my life so you will always be a part of me," he said, walking past her, reminding her that she saved his life after Ole Bay almost killed him. She was also a part-time nurse at a local hospital; so when Ali was brought in, he was half dead due to loss of blood and a low oxygen level. She brought him back to life and helped him get healthy for years; that's how they got close. He even taught her good English which she was now good at.

When he walked out back, she began crying as she walked to the bathroom to get privacy before the nosey guards came snooping.

***

Ali saw Rigo sitting under a tent blocking the bright hot sun rays, drinking grapefruit juice at a glass table full of trays with fruit.

"My friend, glad you're back so soon. I was starting to miss you. Sit please," he said, embracing Ali warmly.

"Glad you feel that way but sorry I took so long. I had to handle business with my casinos. I sold them to a land district under a commercial general liability policy to conceal my investment still, but I plan to open a new casino and I want you to be a part of it," Ali said as Rigo's face went from a smile to a big angry frown.

"What?" he said, confused because opening a new casino will take years to even regain his investment back.

"Don't worry. I can assure you, Rigo, you will be okay but first I have a question. I want you to be honest with me. Who is the woman you sent after my wife?" Ali asked smoothly.

"I don't know what you are assuming," Rigo said, sliding his hand under his chair to pull out a pistol. "Why did it have to come to this? We could have made good money, now look. Your fucking wife killed my family and you were my only way to her, so I plotted it out for years. I know you would need me but I thought you were wiser but you're not. I'm sure I'll find her myself. Now you're no use for me now, Ali." Rigo pointed the gun at his head.

"Remember a queen will always protect her king," Ali said before Rigo's head exploded off his shoulders. As the maid, Longeria, stood there with a smoking gun, Rigo's body dropped as they both looked at each other.

The loud explosion snapped them both out of their trances.

"Boot time, go hide, and thank you!" he said as he heard loud gun fire from inside. The two guards ran in the kitchen running into three bullets apiece in their face.

***

Ayesha wore a black bodycon suit looking sexy with an AR-15 standing over the six dead guards as if it was play time training with her son in the woods.

"You okay, baby?" she said as she saw him approach her. Out of the corner of her eyes she saw a beautiful Spanish woman approach them, making her lift her AR.

"Hold on, she is okay. She saved my life. She is the reason why I'm here," he told Ayesha as she lowered her rifle, not liking the look Longeria was giving her and Ali; she had to walk off before she killed the bitch.

"We got a flight to catch. I'll be outside," she said, walking outside with an attitude as Ali thanked Longeria and left without looking back. Longeria ran upstairs to get Cattolina's daughter she took care of, as she heard her cries. Longeria refused to leave the baby in the house so she planned to raise her herself, plus she took a liking to her.

Chapter Thirty-Five

Fort Worth, Tx

Ole Bay was pulling off the exit into a rest stop in a black Lincoln Towncar with a SUV tailing him ten feet behind. He was on his way back to Mexico. Once he hit El Paso, he knew he would be clear from all danger. Crossing the border was the hard part but one of the Cartel family under him had people on the inside.

The government controlled the border, not the cartel, but Ole Bay trusted his men. Ole Bay had a make-over; he wore a women's dress, fake breasts, a wig and make-up to match his new identity. He knew this was his only way of making it out alive with only very few men.

He was driving for hours; he needed a stop to get something to refuel his energy. The pit stop had a burger king, restroom, and a small convenience store open twenty-four seven. He parked next to two eighteen-wheeler trucks and his goons parked next to him. The long ride had him about to piss on himself.

"I'ma go piss. Order me a number seven, no onions, and hurry the fuck back. We on a time schedule!" Ole Bay told his far best trained men in Spanish, as he walked off in flat heels and a sundress.

On his way to the restroom, a lot of truckers eyed him sexually, thinking he was an ugly hooker looking for a date. Ole Bay was about to walk in the men restroom until it hit him that he was now a woman. He slid into the lady's room, relieved it was empty as he went to take a shit he was holding for hours.

***

Ali and Ayesha were parked on the side of a large double part eighteen-wheeler watching Ole Bay and his crew every move with pistols with silencers on their laps.

The crew had been following Ole Bay for a whole day since he left New Mexico. They caught him coming out of a female clothing store at a shopping center while they were eating lunch in a small

Italian restaurant. Since they came back from Colombia, Ole Bay was their prey and now they got him.

"Which one do you want, love?" Ali asked, watching the old lady walk into the lady restroom but the lady was really their target.

"This motherfucker ruined my family, baby, and I made him a promise," she said as she placed a black Nike hoodie over her head that matched her tracksuit.

"I'ma back you and take care of his puppets," he said, placing the large 50 cal in his hoodie pocket.

***

Ayesha slowly walked to the lady's room, passing families coming out of Burger King with their kids on the road trips and truck drivers.

Once she walked in the bathroom, the strong piss odor hit her as she walked over bloody tampons and dirty tissue. She saw five bathroom stalls; it was a loud hum. She saw big feet with pink toenail polish on the toes and a yellow and green sundress around the person's ankles.

Boom! The stall door kicked in, scaring the life outta Ole Bay as he was finally able to shit at the sight of her gun to his face.

"How did you find me?" he said with a disappointment-laced voice.

"I told you I'll be back," she said, trying to sound like the Terminator, as she laughed. She shot him in his face six times, and his body jerked like fish on land as blood painted the walls.

***

"Right on time," Ali mumbled as the guards were walking in his direction while he was ducked on the side of the GMC truck.

"We got to take a pic of the boss. I can't believe he really dressed like my ex-wife," one of the guards said, taking a sip from his milkshake, looking in the dark sky as the Texas insects attacked their skins.

Before any of them could comment on the joke, Ali popped up and shot one of them in his head. "Cover me—it's a trap," one of the men said as he dropped his food and pulled out a 9mm and started shooting. All three men started shooting towards him, as he shot back while ducking behind the SUV as the alarm went off. Ali caught one of the shooters in his neck twice as he ran between the two eighteen-wheelers as bullets circled him.

Ayesha came out of nowhere and shot the two last gunmen with head shots from a distance as civilians ran inside the store trying to save their life.

"Damn, I told you I had it!" Ali said, pissed off, sweating as if he just ran a marathon in Boston.

"Boy, whatever, I see you still the same. You can't shoot for shit, come on. I know they notified the police," she said, watching all the people staring at them on their phones, even truck drivers.

The Range did ninety out the rest stop as a black Ford Taurus kept a distance on the Range, not knowing what to do because what they saw was not in their plans at all.

The federal agents were watching Ole Bay every move; his case was recently reopened and there was a warrant for his arrest. They planned to bust him at the U.S. border; they even had a team of agents waiting on him.

This was the New Mexican & Arizona task force biggest bust. They even connected with Texas but what they just saw—they were granting a promotion with the Bureau, as they called it in.

***

"Fuck! We got company, baby, and I think it's the pigs; they've been following us ten minutes," he said, looking in his rearview as the Range HD lights brightened up the dark midnight highway.

"I know. Just know I love you," she said, sliding him an AR-15 and loading up her Mack 11 with the drum and coding system attached to it. Seven police cars sped down the highway, coming from both ways, blocking them off as he pulled over as the highway was lit up like a Christmas tree. Agents and state troopers all hopped out, surrounding the truck as six more police cars pulled up.

"Let's do it, babe," Ali said as he hopped out spraying rounds like a madman, as Ayesha followed, lead hitting every target as bullets pierced their teflon vests. After sixty seconds of gun battle, the couple was official and as well as ten police officers, most agents.

***

New Mexico

Cattolina looked sexy in her short red leather Fendi skirt with her Fendi red and black blouse, as she was entering her hotel room. She spent her days hunting down Ayesha, but it was like she was a ghost again but she knew she wasn't too far.

She hadn't been in touch with Rigo because Ayesha was still alive, and she knew he was a man about business and so was she.

As she walked in her hotel room, she wondered why the blinds were closed. It was one p.m. in the afternoon, but she figured it was the hotel maids. Before she stepped six feet in her room, a large metal object slammed into her skull knocking her clean out.

Twenty minutes later she woke up hog-tied to the floor from her wrist to her ankles with her head busted open. She looked up to see a man, but her vision was slightly blurred but when she got a closer look at the man watching the news crying, she knew it was her nephew.

***

Lil Ali almost threw up when he saw pictures of his mother and father gunned down by police.

"What the fuck!" Cattolina said, softly upset her sister let police take her out because she yearned for that day.

Lil Ali held back his tears in deep thought.

"You killed Nicole?" he asked, already knowing the answer.

Nicole's neighbor told him she saw a beautiful woman dressed in a army uniform with foreign feathers come out her house before her murder. Nicole's pregnancy hurt him the worst when he heard about it; that's why he was here.

"You here to play twenty-one questions. You don't look too much like 50 Cent. Let's get this shit over with!" she demanded.

"I guess our bloodline is one of a kind," Lil Ali said as he pointed the draco at her head. There was something about her eyes that froze his trigger finger.

"Kill me please, I'ma poison you if you don't kill me now. I swear I'm going to kill you regardless, so save yourself," Cattolina said seriously as tears rolled down her cheeks.

Lil Ali let off two shots into the bathroom wall behind her head; she didn't blink once.

"Leave the States. If I see you again, I'ma kill you and your child," Lil Ali said, walking out leaving her hog-tied and puzzled.

***

Philly

Abdul and Taqiq sat in his mansion which was heavy guarded by Muslim trained killers at all times. He was heartbroken watching the top stories on the news about the death of two serial killers that was wanted for years by the FBI, CIA, and ATF for over sixty murders.

Taqiq sat on the floor in tears; he knew his parents weren't coming back.

"It will be okay, youngin, trust me, Allah will take care of us. Let's go pray and find your brother," Abdul said, shutting off the TV, looking at Taqiq. He saw something in Taqiq's eyes that he saw before, and it wasn't good.

To Be Continued…
A Gangsta Quran 5

Romell Tukes

Coming Soon

Lock Down Publications and Ca$h Presents assisted publishing packages.

BASIC PACKAGE $499

Editing

Cover Design

Formatting

UPGRADED PACKAGE $800

Typing

Editing

Cover Design

Formatting

ADVANCE PACKAGE $1,200

Typing

Editing

Cover Design

Formatting

Copyright registration

Romell Tukes

Proofreading

Upload book to Amazon

LDP SUPREME PACKAGE $1,500

Typing

Editing

Cover Design

Formatting

Copyright registration

Proofreading

Set up Amazon account

Upload book to Amazon

Advertise on LDP Amazon and Facebook page

***Other services available upon request. Additional charges
may apply

Lock Down Publications

P.O. Box 944

Stockbridge, GA 30281-9998

Phone # 470 303-9761

Submission Guideline

Submit the first three chapters of your completed manuscript to ldpsubmissions@gmail.com, subject line: Your book's title. The manuscript must be in a .dcc file and sent as an attachment. Document should be in Times New Roman, double spaced and in size 12 font. Also, provide your synopsis and full contact information. If sending multiple submissions, they must each be in a separate email.

Have a story but no way to send it electronically? You can still submit to LDP/Ca$h Presents. Send in the first three chapters, written or typed, of your completed manuscript to:

LDP: Submissions Dept
Po Box 944
Stockbridge, Ga 30281

DO NOT send original manuscript. Must be a duplicate.

Provide your synopsis and a cover letter containing your full contact information.

Thanks for considering LDP and Ca$h Presents.

NEW RELEASES

JACK BOYS VS DOPE BOYS by ROMELL TUKES
KILLA KOUNTY 2 by KHUFU
IN A HUSTLER I TRUST by MONET DRAGUN
THE COCAINE PRINCESS by KING RIO
TOE TAGZ 4 by AH'MILLION
A GANGSTA'S QUR'AN by ROMELL TUKES

KINGPIN KILLAZ IV

STREET KINGS III

PAID IN BLOOD III

CARTEL KILLAZ IV

DOPE GODS III

Hood Rich

SINS OF A HUSTLA II

ASAD

RICH $AVAGE II

MONEY IN THE GRAVE II

By Martell Troublesome Bolden

YAYO V

Bred In The Game 2

S. Allen

CREAM III

By Yolanda Moore

SON OF A DOPE FIEND III

HEAVEN GOT A GHETTO II

By Renta

LOYALTY AIN'T PROMISED III

By Keith Williams

I'M NOTHING WITHOUT HIS LOVE II

SINS OF A THUG II

TO THE THUG I LOVED BEFORE II

IN A HUSTLER I TRUST II

By Monet Dragun

QUIET MONEY IV

EXTENDED CLIP III

THUG LIFE IV

By **Trai'Quan**

THE STREETS MADE ME IV

By **Larry D. Wright**

IF YOU CROSS ME ONCE II

By **Anthony Fields**

THE STREETS WILL NEVER CLOSE II

By K'ajji

HARD AND RUTHLESS III

THE BILLIONAIRE BENTLEYS II

Von Diesel

KILLA KOUNTY III

By Khufu

MONEY GAME III

By Smoove Dolla

JACK BOYS VS DOPE BOYS II

A GANGSTA'S QUR'AN V

By Romell Tukes

MURDA WAS THE CASE II

Elijah R. Freeman

THE STREETS NEVER LET GO II

By Robert Baptiste

AN UNFORESEEN LOVE III

By **Meesha**

KING OF THE TRENCHES III

by **GHOST & TRANAY ADAMS**

MONEY MAFIA II

LOYAL TO THE SOIL II

By **Jibril Williams**

QUEEN OF THE ZOO II

By **Black Migo**

THE BRICK MAN IV

THE COCAINE PRINCESS II
By King Rio
VICIOUS LOYALTY II
By Kingpen
A GANGSTA'S PAIN II
By J-Blunt
CONFESSIONS OF A JACKBOY III
By Nicholas Lock
GRIMEY WAYS II
By Ray Vinci
KING KILLA II
By Vincent "Vitto" Holloway

Available Now

RESTRAINING ORDER **I & II**
By **CA$H & Coffee**
LOVE KNOWS NO BOUNDARIES **I II & III**
By **Coffee**
RAISED AS A GOON I, II, III & IV
BRED BY THE SLUMS I, II, III
BLAST FOR ME I & II
ROTTEN TO THE CORE I II III
A BRONX TALE I, II, III

DUFFLE BAG CARTEL I II III IV V VI

HEARTLESS GOON I II III IV V

A SAVAGE DOPEBOY I II

DRUG LORDS I II III

CUTTHROAT MAFIA I II

KING OF THE TRENCHES

By **Ghost**

LAY IT DOWN **I & II**

LAST OF A DYING BREED I II

BLOOD STAINS OF A SHOTTA I & II III

By **Jamaica**

LOYAL TO THE GAME I II III

LIFE OF SIN I, II III

By **TJ & Jelissa**

BLOODY COMMAS I & II

SKI MASK CARTEL I II & III

KING OF NEW YORK I II,III IV V

RISE TO POWER I II III

COKE KINGS I II III IV V

BORN HEARTLESS I II III IV

KING OF THE TRAP I II

By **T.J. Edwards**

IF LOVING HIM IS WRONG…I & II

LOVE ME EVEN WHEN IT HURTS I II III

By **Jelissa**

WHEN THE STREETS CLAP BACK I & II III

THE HEART OF A SAVAGE I II III

MONEY MAFIA

LOYAL TO THE SOIL

By **Jibril Williams**

229

A DISTINGUISHED THUG STOLE MY HEART I II & III

LOVE SHOULDN'T HURT I II III IV

RENEGADE BOYS I II III IV

PAID IN KARMA I II III

SAVAGE STORMS I II

AN UNFORESEEN LOVE I II

By **Meesha**

A GANGSTER'S CODE I &, II III

A GANGSTER'S SYN I II III

THE SAVAGE LIFE I II III

CHAINED TO THE STREETS I II III

BLOOD ON THE MONEY I II III

A GANGSTA'S PAIN

By J-Blunt

PUSH IT TO THE LIMIT

By **Bre' Hayes**

BLOOD OF A BOSS **I, II, III, IV, V**

SHADOWS OF THE GAME

TRAP BASTARD

By **Askari**

THE STREETS BLEED MURDER **I, II & III**

THE HEART OF A GANGSTA I II& III

By **Jerry Jackson**

CUM FOR ME I II III IV V VI VII VIII

An **LDP Erotica Collaboration**

BRIDE OF A HUSTLA **I II & II**

THE FETTI GIRLS **I, II& III**

CORRUPTED BY A GANGSTA I, II III, IV

BLINDED BY HIS LOVE

THE PRICE YOU PAY FOR LOVE I, II ,III

DOPE GIRL MAGIC I II III
By **Destiny Skai**
WHEN A GOOD GIRL GOES BAD
By **Adrienne**
THE COST OF LOYALTY I II III
By Kweli
A GANGSTER'S REVENGE **I II III & IV**
THE BOSS MAN'S DAUGHTERS I II III IV V
A SAVAGE LOVE **I & II**
BAE BELONGS TO ME I II
A HUSTLER'S DECEIT I, II, III
WHAT BAD BITCHES DO I, II, III
SOUL OF A MONSTER I II III
KILL ZONE
A DOPE BOY'S QUEEN I II III
By **Aryanna**
A KINGPIN'S AMBITON
A KINGPIN'S AMBITION **II**
I MURDER FOR THE DOUGH
By **Ambitious**
TRUE SAVAGE I II III IV V VI VII
DOPE BOY MAGIC I, II, III
MIDNIGHT CARTEL I II III
CITY OF KINGZ I II
NIGHTMARE ON SILENT AVE
THE PLUG OF LIL MEXICO II

By **Chris Green**
A DOPEBOY'S PRAYER
By **Eddie "Wolf" Lee**

THE KING CARTEL **I, II & III**

By **Frank Gresham**

THESE NIGGAS AIN'T LOYAL **I, II & III**

By **Nikki Tee**

GANGSTA SHYT **I II &III**

By **CATO**

THE ULTIMATE BETRAYAL

By **Phoenix**

BOSS'N UP **I , II & III**

By **Royal Nicole**

I LOVE YOU TO DEATH

By **Destiny J**

I RIDE FOR MY HITTA

I STILL RIDE FOR MY HITTA

By **Misty Holt**

LOVE & CHASIN' PAPER

By **Qay Crockett**

TO DIE IN VAIN

SINS OF A HUSTLA

By **ASAD**

BROOKLYN HUSTLAZ

By **Boogsy Morina**

BROOKLYN ON LOCK I & II

By **Sonovia**

GANGSTA CITY

By **Teddy Duke**

A DRUG KING AND HIS DIAMOND I & II III

A DOPEMAN'S RICHES

HER MAN, MINE'S TOO I, II

CASH MONEY HO'S

THE WIFEY I USED TO BE I II
By Nicole Goosby
TRAPHOUSE KING **I II & III**
KINGPIN KILLAZ I II III
STREET KINGS I II
PAID IN BLOOD **I II**
CARTEL KILLAZ I II III
DOPE GODS I II
By **Hood Rich**
LIPSTICK KILLAH **I, II, III**
CRIME OF PASSION I II & III
FRIEND OR FOE I II III
By **Mimi**
STEADY MOBBN' **I, II, III**
THE STREETS STAINED MY SOUL I II III
By **Marcellus Allen**
WHO SHOT YA **I, II, III**
SON OF A DOPE FIEND I II
HEAVEN GOT A GHETTO
Renta
GORILLAZ IN THE BAY **I II III IV**
TEARS OF A GANGSTA I II
3X KRAZY I II
STRAIGHT BEAST MODE
DE'KARI
TRIGGADALE I II III
MURDAROBER WAS THE CASE
Elijah R. Freeman
GOD BLESS THE TRAPPERS I, II, III
THESE SCANDALOUS STREETS I, II, III

Romell Tukes

FEAR MY GANGSTA I, II, III IV, V

THESE STREETS DON'T LOVE NOBODY I, II

BURY ME A G I, II, III, IV, V

A GANGSTA'S EMPIRE I, II, III, IV

THE DOPEMAN'S BODYGAURD I II

THE REALEST KILLAZ I II III

THE LAST OF THE OGS I II III

Tranay Adams

THE STREETS ARE CALLING

Duquie Wilson

MARRIED TO A BOSS I II III

By Destiny Skai & Chris Green

KINGZ OF THE GAME I II III IV V VI

Playa Ray

SLAUGHTER GANG I II III

RUTHLESS HEART I II III

By Willie Slaughter

FUK SHYT

By Blakk Diamond

DON'T F#CK WITH MY HEART I II

By Linnea

ADDICTED TO THE DRAMA I II III

IN THE ARM OF HIS BOSS II

By Jamila

YAYO I II III IV

A SHOOTER'S AMBITION I II

BRED IN THE GAME

By S. Allen

TRAP GOD I II III

RICH $AVAGE

MONEY IN THE GRAVE I II

By Martell Troublesome Bolden

FOREVER GANGSTA

GLOCKS ON SATIN SHEETS I II

By Adrian Dulan

TOE TAGZ I II III IV

LEVELS TO THIS SHYT I II

By Ah'Million

KINGPIN DREAMS I II III

By Paper Boi Rari

CONFESSIONS OF A GANGSTA I II III IV

CONFESSIONS OF A JACKBOY I II

By Nicholas Lock

I'M NOTHING WITHOUT HIS LOVE

SINS OF A THUG

TO THE THUG I LOVED BEFORE

A GANGSTA SAVED XMAS

IN A HUSTLER I TRUST

By Monet Dragun

CAUGHT UP IN THE LIFE I II III

THE STREETS NEVER LET GO

By Robert Baptiste

NEW TO THE GAME I II III

MONEY, MURDER & MEMORIES I II III

By **Malik D. Rice**

LIFE OF A SAVAGE I II III

A GANGSTA'S QUR'AN I II III IV

MURDA SEASON I II III

GANGLAND CARTEL I II III

CHI'RAQ GANGSTAS I II III

KILLERS ON ELM STREET I II III

JACK BOYZ N DA BRONX I II III

A DOPEBOY'S DREAM I II III

JACK BOYS VS DOPE BOYS

By **Romell Tukes**

LOYALTY AIN'T PROMISED I II

By Keith Williams

QUIET MONEY I II III

THUG LIFE I II III

EXTENDED CLIP I II

By **Trai'Quan**

THE STREETS MADE ME I II III

By **Larry D. Wright**

THE ULTIMATE SACRIFICE I, II, III, IV, V, VI

KHADIFI

IF YOU CROSS ME ONCE

ANGEL I II

IN THE BLINK OF AN EYE

By **Anthony Fields**

THE LIFE OF A HOOD STAR

By Ca$h & Rashia Wilson

THE STREETS WILL NEVER CLOSE

By K'ajji

CREAM I II

By Yolanda Moore

NIGHTMARES OF A HUSTLA I II III

By King Dream

CONCRETE KILLA I II

VICIOUS LOYALTY

By Kingpen

HARD AND RUTHLESS I II

MOB TOWN 251

THE BILLIONAIRE BENTLEYS

By Von Diesel

GHOST MOB

Stilloan Robinson

MOB TIES I II III IV V

By SayNoMore

BODYMORE MURDERLAND I II III

By Delmont Player

FOR THE LOVE OF A BOSS

By C. D. Blue

MOBBED UP I II III IV

THE BRICK MAN I II III

THE COCAINE PRINCESS

By King Rio

KILLA KOUNTY I II

By Khufu

MONEY GAME I II

By Smoove Dolla

A GANGSTA'S KARMA I II

By FLAME

KING OF THE TRENCHES I II

by **GHOST & TRANAY ADAMS**

QUEEN OF THE ZOO

By **Black Migo**

GRIMEY WAYS

By Ray Vinci

XMAS WITH AN ATL SHOOTER

By Ca$h & Destiny Skai

KING KILLA

By Vincent "Vitto" Holloway

BOOKS BY LDP'S CEO, CA$H

TRUST IN NO MAN

TRUST IN NO MAN 2

TRUST IN NO MAN 3

BONDED BY BLOOD

SHORTY GOT A THUG

THUGS CRY

THUGS CRY 2

THUGS CRY 3

TRUST NO BITCH

TRUST NO BITCH 2

TRUST NO BITCH 3

TIL MY CASKET DROPS

RESTRAINING ORDER

RESTRAINING ORDER 2

IN LOVE WITH A CONVICT

LIFE OF A HOOD STAR

XMAS WITH AN ATL SHOOTER

Romell Tukes